# THE TEST

# THE TEST

## TAWNA FENSKE

Entangled Publishing, LLC
10940 S Parker Rd
Suite 327
Parker, CO 80134
rights@entangledpublishing.com

Scorched is an imprint of Entangled Publishing, LLC.

Edited by Liz Pelletier
Cover design by LJ Anderson
Cover art by Dragosh Co/Shutterstock

Manufactured in the United States of America

First Edition February 2018

entangled
scorched

*For editor Liz.*
*Because you let me keep the alley sex.*
*And also because you make my books a zillion times better.*
*But mostly for the alley sex.*

# Chapter One

LISA

"I'll have the Barbadian Secret martini, but with Hendrick's gin instead of the Aria, and I'd prefer the grapefruit-shishido shrub instead of the tarragon, please."

I smile at the cocktail waitress, who nods and jots something on her notepad. "No problem."

"I know I'm fussy," I tell her in a half-conspiratorial, half-apologetic tone that wins more kindness from servers than my extra-generous tips. "But it's always fabulous when you make it that way."

She gives me a friendly wink. "Coming right up."

"Oh, and if you have kaffir leaves," I add, "I'd really prefer that over the lime zest garnish."

"Jesus, Lisa." Across the table, my sister, Cassie, rolls her eyes. "Are you ordering a cocktail or buying a luxury car?"

Our other sister, Missy, pats Cassie's hand with a haughty expression I suspect mirrors the one I routinely throw at our younger sister. "There's a real art to craft cocktails," Missy informs her. "You can't blame her for knowing exactly what she wants."

I smile at Missy for having my back, but also at Cassie for being—well, Cassie. My polar opposite in most ways, but I love her more than Proenza Schouler's new spring line of dresses, and that's saying something.

I'm also determined to help the poor lamb plan her wedding. "So, Cassie," I say as I pop one of the Driftwood Room's famous Sizzling Forest Mushrooms into my mouth and chew. "Did you decide on the letterpress or the foil stamping for your save the date cards?"

She looks at me as though I've just shoved cocktail straws up my nostrils and pretended to be a walrus. "I'm a soil scientist getting married," she says. "Not a senator sending correspondence to foreign dignitaries."

Her expression softens almost imperceptibly, and she exchanges a look with Missy. I'd bet my favorite pair of Louboutins that our older sister just stepped on her foot under the table, and I know why.

I sigh and address the elephant in the room. "I'm fine, you two. I don't mind wedding chit-chat. *Please.* It's been six months since Gary pulled the disappearing groom act. I'm better off without him, obviously."

"Obviously," they chorus, Cassie sounding more convinced than Missy. There's that look again.

I ignore it and glance toward the bar, wondering what's taking so long for the drinks. Blocking my view of the bartender is a hulking figure in a black T-shirt, with tattoos covering both arms. I can't see his face, but his shoulders look like he spends his spare time bench-pressing SUVs. His ass is a work of art, too, like a chiseled piece of granite fitted with well-worn denim.

"Is the limp-dicked fucker still in Arizona for that men's retreat thing?"

I snap my attention back to Cassie, momentarily confused. "What?"

Seeing my confusion, Cassie glances toward the bar. When her gaze lands on Granite Ass, she gives a knowing smirk. "I was asking about Gary, but I like the look of anti-Gary much better."

Missy frowns and peers around Cassie. "Anti-Gary? Oh. *Oh.* Wow. That guy's huge."

"Stop staring." I swat at both of them as Granite Ass turns and catches me watching him. My breath snags in my throat, and it takes five full seconds for me to figure out how to look away. In that time, I'm hypnotized by the most stunning, icy-blue eyes I've ever seen in my life.

"Here come the drinks," I announce in a voice that doesn't sound like mine at all. It's high and quivery like one of those porno girls in the videos I used to catch Gary watching. "Bottoms up, girls."

I snatch a frosted martini glass off the tray hovering next to my head. The waitress starts to say something as I take a big gulp, then sputter.

"Guh!" I gasp. "That's not the Barbadian Secret martini."

The waitress stares at me like I've just belched in public. "I'm sorry, ma'am—that's the order for the next table," she says. "Yours will be here in just a second."

Heat creeps into my cheeks, and I'm not sure if it's from embarrassment or from the extra-strong drink.

Or the fact that everyone's staring at me, Granite Ass included. I'm deliberately not looking, but I can feel those blue eyes drilling into the side of my head.

Determined to salvage my dignity, I offer an apologetic wave to the befuddled-looking couple at the next table. "I'm so sorry," I say. "Your next round is on me. My apologies."

Then I take a daintier sip of the drink, tasting it for real this time. My taste buds perk up, reveling in the icy contrast between brine and bitter. I sip again, and a fat olive stuffed with bleu cheese bumps my lip.

"What on earth is this?" I ask. "It's amazing."

"A dirty martini," the waitress offers. "Extra dirty, actually."

I sip again, entranced by the unfamiliar mix of flavors. It's salty and sharp with tiny flecks of ice swirling in a gin mixture that smells like juniper berries. "It's incredible."

Missy stares at me like I've just announced a fondness for Cheetos. "That's basically the opposite of what you ordered."

Cassie smirks. "Maybe she ought to try opposites more often."

I take another sip, considering her words. How did I never realize there was this whole other realm of cocktail possibilities? Savory instead of sweet, salty instead of fruity.

"Is this seriously the first time you've tried a dirty martini?" Cassie asks.

I roll my eyes and sip my new drink again. "I've never had a dirty martini. I'm an interior designer, not a soil scientist like you."

It's Missy's turn to look perplexed. "I'm not a soil scientist, either, but even I've had a dirty martini."

I sigh and set my drink down, regarding my sisters with exaggerated patience. "I've had plenty of martinis, as you well know. Is it really so peculiar that I've never tried it dirty?"

"That's a shame." A low male voice close to my ear makes me jump, and I turn to see Granite Ass has slid in to the seat beside me. Those icy-blue eyes bore into mine, registering some strange combination of amusement and lust with an odd hint of aggression. What's that about?

"Sounds like that's something you ought to remedy," he murmurs.

The timbre of his voice makes me shiver, and I'm not sure we're still talking about drinks. I stare at him, at a complete loss for words. He's even bigger up close, and I wonder how he managed to move from his barstool into my space without me noticing. He's staring like he can see right through my dress, and the thought doesn't trouble me as much as it ought to.

I swallow and taste olive brine on the back of my tongue. Somewhere in my brain, my sister's words echo in my head.

*Maybe she ought to try opposites more often.*

She's right, dammit. I'm a thirty-one-year-old single woman whose ex-fiancé's silk ties are still folded neatly in the dresser drawer where he left them. How the hell did I end up here?

My whole life flickers before my eyes in a grainy, ten-second film. A life filled with wine clubs and yacht parties and impeccably tasteful drapes.

Maybe every life choice I've made so far—drinks, dates, everything in between—has been the wrong one. Maybe my instincts are so far off-kilter that the only fix is to do the exact *opposite* of what my gut tells me to.

These are crazy thoughts to be having in a Portland hipster bar on a random Tuesday evening. My gut roils with a potent brew of gin, adrenaline, and lust, so trusting it right now isn't an option.

But there's one thing I do know.

Granite Ass is making more than my taste buds tingle.

"Well, then," I tell him, pausing to lick my lips. "I don't suppose you'd be the guy to teach me a thing or two about learning to like it dirty?"

# Chapter Two

## Dax

*Holy fucking shit.*

How did I even get here?

One second I'm sitting across the bar from my snotty ex-girlfriend, Kaitlyn, thinking about how badly I'd like to rub her face in my recent career success and the fact that my life is pretty fucking awesome since she walked out.

The next second I'm sidling up next to Kaitlyn and realizing *holymotherofhell*, this isn't Kaitlyn at all.

It's another polished blonde with a dress that spells "money," a calculating look that spells "trouble," and a body that spells "sin."

That's an awful lot of spelling for a guy who barely finished high school and never went to college. Not that it's stopped me from busting ass to make something of myself. To go from a grubby kid scrounging for scrap metal in his daddy's junkyard, to a minimum wage steelworker, to the guy who holds the patent on a double steel-walled beverage container that's made me filthy fucking rich in the last year.

Where was I?

Right, the blonde. The one who's looking at me like she wants to pour maple syrup on my abs and devour me like a stack of flapjacks. What the hell just happened?

"Dax," I manage to spit out. "Dax Kensington. And you are?"

"Lisa Michaels." She extends a manicured hand, and I'm not sure if I'm supposed to kiss it or shake it. I settle for the handshake, then notice my knuckles are grease-stained from working on my bike this morning. Fuck.

Lisa notices, too, but instead of gasping with prissy horror and drawing her hand back, she meets my eyes again and gives me that calculating smile.

"Dax," she says. "What do you do for fun?"

It's not the question I expected from her. Not "what do you do for a living" or "do you prefer mutual funds or blue-chip stocks," and it takes me a moment to answer.

"Well, I'm really into competitive duck herding, but I also enjoy train-surfing and extreme ironing."

It's a dickhead answer, not just because I'm being a jackass, but because I'm guessing the ironing thing isn't too far off the mark of what Lisa Michaels really does for fun. Her outfit looks like she gets up to press it once an hour to eliminate unsightly wrinkles.

She surprises me by tossing all that shiny gold hair and laughing. "Oh, you're a real smart-ass, hmm? You seem like a man who needs to be taught manners."

Across the table, Lisa's two companions exchange a worried glance. One of them clears her throat and gives me an apologetic look. "Our sister is, um…going through a rough time."

The other one nods at Lisa. "And she's not really used to drinks that are quite so…stiff."

Is it my imagination, or did that chick just glance at my

crotch? I don't have time to ponder it because Lisa's talking again, and damn if the woman doesn't yank my attention like she's got it on a choke chain.

"My sisters are right," she says as she picks up her martini and takes a ladylike sip. "But I suppose one could posit that there hasn't been nearly enough *stiff* or *dirty* in my life thus far."

Did she really just say "posit" and "thus" in the same sentence as "stiff" and "dirty?" Who the hell is this chick? And why the fuck do I care?

I tap the stem of her martini glass. "How many of those have you had?"

She sets it down on the table, reaches under the table and grabs my knee. Her green eyes lock with mine, and it shocks me enough that I almost drop my beer.

"Enough to take you home with me right now and do unspeakable things all night long." She frowns, possibly replaying those words in her head and not liking the sound of them. "Wait, I didn't mean to imply I'd have to be drunk in order to—"

"One," her sister interjects, smiling a little as she shakes her head. "Lisa has only had the one drink."

"And no, she's not crazy," the other sister adds helpfully, tossing out the sort of fond smile you'd reserve for a nutty aunt who just gnawed the drumstick off the turkey at Thanksgiving dinner. "Present display notwithstanding."

Lisa shoots them a disdainful look, but there's more warmth in it than actual anger. It's clear these three are tight. I'm still a little mind-whacked from her hand on my knee and the words she just said a few seconds ago.

*Enough to take you home with me right now and do unspeakable things all night long.*

"I'm sorry, did you just proposition me?" I ask.

Lisa nods, looking a little surprised by it herself. "Yes.

Yes, I did. Is that a problem?"

I think about it a second. "You're not married?"

"Of course not." She gives me a haughty eyebrow lift.

"Or drunk?"

She scoffs. "Hardly."

I study her, trying to figure out the angle. "Is this some sort of grudge fuck?"

She looks me right in the eye, an unexpected challenge in those green depths. "Would that be a problem for you?"

I hesitate. Do I really want to start down this path? True, I have a weakness for polished blondes, but that hasn't turned out great for me in the past.

Then again, I did come over here intending to one-up my ex.

Lisa's hand slides a few inches up my thigh, and I find myself grunting an answer. "Nope. Grudge fucks are not a problem."

Her face breaks into a broad smile, and my chest tightens unexpectedly. Holy hell, she's gorgeous when she does that. I grip my beer and remind myself to keep a tight grip on my sanity while I'm at it.

"Well, Dax Kensington," Lisa says, licking her lips. "Shall we get out of here?"

# Chapter Three

## LISA

Does it count as false bravado if I really, really *want* to be the sort of brave, confident, sexy woman who'd bring a tattooed bad boy home for a one-night stand?

This, and other thoughts, are whirling through my brain as I unlock the front door to my condo and usher Dax inside. "Pardon the mess," I tell him, breathing in the pleasant scent of pomegranate and mission fig wafting from the Pottery Barn diffuser on the credenza. "I wasn't expecting company."

Dax steps into my living room and turns a slow circle, a bit like a bull in a china shop. A really big, virile bull. I swallow hard as he turns back to face me.

"This looks like something out of a home decorating magazine," he says. "Where exactly is the mess?"

I frown and hustle forward to straighten the coffee table book that's at a 65-degree angle instead of a 45-degree angle. There's also a teaspoon in the sink from my morning Earl Grey, and I rush over to load it in the dishwasher.

It occurs to me this is not how most women kick off an episode of wild, no-strings sex.

"Sorry," I say, not sure if I'm apologizing for the teaspoon or the fact that I'm behaving like Martha Stewart on speed. "I'm, uh…a little new at this."

He studies me a moment, those icy-blue eyes assessing. Then he nods. "Look, we don't have to do anything if that was all a show for your sisters."

"What?"

He shrugs and offers a heartbreakingly kind look, which is sooo different from the smoldering gaze he should be giving a woman he wants to shag silly. God, I'm blowing this.

"I get it," he says as he leans back against the wall of my foyer, the sympathy in his eyes making me want to hide under the dining room table. "I promise you won't hurt my feelings if that was just an act for Missy and Cassie. How about I give you a hickey for proof, and then I'll be on my way. You'll never have to see me again."

I'm touched that he'd offer something like that. Okay, maybe not the hickey. Still, it shows he's concerned about me. That he's giving me a chance to change my mind or back out. Or wait. Is he the one who wants to back out?

Determined to take the bull—the very virile bull—by the horns, I smooth my hands down the front of my Diane von Furstenberg pencil skirt and square my shoulders.

"I can assure you, I totally want to screw." I wince at my own words, feeling heat creep into my cheeks. "People don't say that, do they?"

Dax shakes his head, a bemused glint in his eye. There's a sexiness in his smile that wasn't there five seconds ago, and my pulse ticks up a notch. "People don't generally say that," he confirms. "Doesn't mean it wasn't hot as hell, though."

I take a shaky breath and wonder what happened to my bravado. It seems to be evaporating now that I'm here in my home revealing how very uncool I am. "Um, look—could we maybe sit and…uh, talk first, or something?"

He laughs and pushes himself off the wall. He moves closer to me, close enough to brush the tips of my fingers with his knuckles. He takes my right hand in his, then the left, making goose bumps prickle all the way up my arms.

"For the record," he says, "it's not my MO to pounce on a woman the second I walk through the door. Not unless she asks me to."

The fact that he phrased it that way sends a funny shudder of relief through me. I'm not sure if it's because I like knowing one of us has some experience here, or that I appreciate the acknowledgment that I'm calling the shots. That I have the right to say no at any time.

But "no" is the last thing on my mind as he strokes my knuckles with the pad of one oversized thumb. It's gentle and warm, and I'm not even sure he knows he's doing it. The gesture is almost as soothing as the earthy, sagebrush scent of his cologne or aftershave or deodorant or whatever the hell it is. Maybe it's just Dax. In any case, my shoulders start to unclench.

"I'm sorry, where are my manners?" I clear my throat and take a half-step toward the kitchen. "Let me just pour us some wine—"

"Nope," he says, tightening his hold on my hands. He looks deep into my eyes, and I suppress a shiver. "That's my one rule," he says. "If you need a buzz to go through with this, I'm not the guy for the job."

I nod, thrilled by his take-charge approach. Gary was never like that. Dax is right, of course. If I'm going to do this, I should be fully aware of what I'm choosing. Fully committed to this act of debauchery.

*Do wanton women use words like debauchery? Or wanton?*

"How about Perrier?" I offer, determined to be a good hostess. "I also have Evian or La Croix if you prefer."

Dax frowns. "Can I just get some water?"

I start to point out that those were all different types of water, but maybe he knows this. Maybe he wants to see if I'm the sort of spontaneous girl who can be wild and crazy and drink straight-up tap water.

*Oh my God, shut up.*

I swallow hard and try my best to appear cool and composed.

"Lisa?"

"Yeah?"

"Is there a reason you're gripping my hand like you're trying to squeeze juice out of a grapefruit?"

I look down to see he's right. I'm like a freaking anaconda. I drop his hand like it's on fire. "I'm sorry, I'm just a little nervous."

He smiles and takes my hand back, then reaches for the other. Now we're standing here in the middle of my living room holding hands like two four-year-olds playing ring-around-the-rosie.

This is *so* not how I imagined my first no-strings hookup.

"Close your eyes." His voice is low and soothing, and I obey without hesitation. I don't even ask why.

"Very good." Something about his gentle baritone makes my heart slow from a gallop to a canter.

"Breathe in through your nose," he says softly. "Inhale for a count of one...two...three...four...five...six." His voice is steady, unhurried, and his hands are warm around mine.

I do exactly what he says. I swear I'd jump off my roof right now as long as he ordered me to do it in this velvet-edged, milk-chocolaty voice.

"Now exhale for a count of eight...seven...six...five... four...three...two...one," he murmurs. "That's it. Good girl."

He's breathing with me, I can tell. My eyes are still closed, but he's so close I can sense the rise and fall of his chest. Is this foreplay? I have no idea. Gary's idea of foreplay was muting the ten o'clock news and patting the mattress beside him. Don't think I didn't notice how he'd peer at the stock market crawl over my shoulder.

"You're breathing fast again," Dax says, jarring me back to the moment. "Focus on breathing in slowly through your nose for six breaths. Then out for eight. Always more breaths going out than in."

"How do you know this?" I ask.

My eyes are still closed, but I feel his hands tense in mine. "Practiced a lot of self-soothing as a kid."

There's a gruffness to his voice that wasn't there a few minutes ago, and I start to open my eyes. But Dax gives my fingers a gentle squeeze and keeps counting.

"In for one…two…three…four…five…six," he murmurs.

How many minutes pass? Maybe only a few seconds. I could stand here forever, holding hands with this man, breathing in and out and feeling my own heartbeat slow.

Finally, I open my eyes and look at him. His blue eyes are watchful, curious.

"Answer me this," I say. "Is this the lamest entrée to casual sex you've ever had in your life?"

He grins and lets go of my hands.

"Grab the water," he says. "I'll meet you on the sofa."

Then he turns and walks through the living room, leaving me to wonder what the hell just happened.

# Chapter Four

## Dax

Lisa returns to the living room with two lemon-sliced glasses of ice water on a sterling silver tray, and as I watch her hips sway, I replay her last question in my mind.

*Is this the lamest entrée to casual sex you've ever had in your life?*

"For the record, you're not lame," I tell her as she sits down beside me and hands me a glass of water. "You're actually pretty cute."

"Cute," she repeats, spitting out the word like a piece of gristle. "I'm not trying to be cute. I'm aiming for sexy, wild, and sophisticated."

I grin and take a sip of water. "And you're nailing two out of three."

She doesn't ask which one she's missing. I'm guessing she knows, but I'm also guessing there's something she doesn't.

It wouldn't take much to bring out Lisa Michaels's wild side.

I can see it in her eyes. There's a lust-fueled superheroine behind that pearl choker and silk blouse. The thought of uncovering her sends my dick throbbing.

But first things first.

"So, your sister said you're going through a tough time," I begin. "And you mentioned a grudge fuck," I add. "Tell me more."

She stares at me for a moment, then folds her hands primly on her lap. "Gary and I dated for four years, got engaged at the three-year mark, and had planned a perfect June wedding."

"I take it that didn't happen?"

She shakes her head, and I watch her eyes for signs that she's not over the guy. I'm not seeing them, but it isn't like I know her that well.

"He pulled a no-show at the wedding," she says, pressing her lips together in a thin line before continuing. "On the bright side, it left me with six cases of Dom Pérignon to enjoy by myself."

"Not all in one sitting, I hope?"

She laughs and shakes her head. "No, of course not. And I really am over him. I promise. It's just—"

Her brow furrows as she searches for the right conclusion to that sentence. I find I really want to know, really want to hear what she's thinking. It's been a long time since I hung on a woman's words like this.

"Any guy who'd pull a stunt like that is a loser," I tell her. "You deserve better."

"I suppose so," she says, scratching at a nonexistent spot on her skirt with one perfectly manicured nail. "But then again, I'm the loser who thought I wanted to marry him."

I start to say something comforting, but Lisa stops scratching and looks up at me. "You know what Gary said to me after his friend, Preston, caught his girlfriend cheating with the woman she and Preston had a threesome with?"

It takes me a moment to digest that, both the logistics of what she's saying and the fact that Lisa just uttered the word "threesome."

"What did Gary say?" I ask.

"He said, 'I'm glad I never have to worry about craziness like that with you, Lisa.'"

I nod, though I'm not entirely sure what the correct response is here. "I'm sure he meant it as a compliment." I'm not actually trying to defend the guy, just trying to make Lisa feel less shitty. "He knew you were loyal and trustworthy."

She gives me a withering look and picks up her own glass of water. "That's also how you'd describe a Labrador retriever."

I start to argue, but she waves a hand.

"It's not that I'm mad about that. I mean, he probably had a point." She doesn't break eye contact, but seems to hesitate. I wait for her to finish, to form whatever thought is on her mind.

"Have you ever woken up one day and realized that maybe your gut has been steering you wrong all along?" she asks. "Like you thought you wanted one thing, and you made all these decisions to get there, but it turns out that's not what you wanted at all?"

A big ball of iron coils up in the pit of my stomach, but I push it aside and nod. "Yeah. I think I know what you're saying."

"I want something different. Something that's the total opposite of what I'm used to."

"And that's me?"

"Maybe. For tonight anyway." She gives a nervous little laugh and tosses her hair. "I guess I just feel like maybe I've missed out on doing a few things. And maybe guys like you are one of them."

"Guys like me," I repeat, forcing myself to keep an even voice. "How do you mean that?"

I watch her face, braced for the words.

*Dumb. Low-class. Unsophisticated.*

"Hot." She blinks like she's surprised herself with the word, then grins. "Big. Strong. A little rough around the edges, but in a sexy way."

It's my turn to be surprised, and I buy myself a few seconds by reaching out to tuck a strand of hair behind her ear. "Thank you."

"You're welcome."

I let my hand linger by her ear, admiring the perfect shell of it. Pearl studs glisten on her lobes, and I wonder what it would feel like to run my tongue from there to the base of her throat.

"For what it's worth," I murmur. "Gary doesn't know what the hell he's talking about."

"Oh?"

"You're smokin' hot."

She smiles, but it's a little uncertain. "Thank you."

"Like, seriously hot. Hotter than a non-consumable tungsten electrode used in gas-tungsten arc welding."

"*What?*" She bursts out laughing, throwing her whole body forward and bumping my forearm with her breast. Every nerve in my body flickers to life.

I expect her to pull back, but instead, she leans into me. Her thigh moves against mine, and my breath catches in my throat as her skirt hikes up three inches.

"Welding," I say, almost forgetting what we were talking about. "That's a type of high temperature welding used for things like motorcycle or bike repair."

"You're a welder?"

I can't tell if there's judgment or intrigue in the question, so I decide not to answer for now. I like having her this close, feeling the weight of her thigh on mine. Her breast still brushes my bicep, and I resist the urge to press against it.

"You're also hotter than a molten weld puddle shielded by an argon/carbon dioxide mix in flux-cored arc welding," I murmur.

"Molten weld puddle and—what?"

The question comes out a little breathless, and I notice the flutter of her pulse in the hollow of her throat. She's staring at me like she can't believe the words coming out of my mouth.

Neither can I.

"It's another type of welding used for thicker materials or steel erections," I say and watch her lips part. "Also, very hot," I add.

"I—oh." She shifts on the sofa, a funny little squirm that brings her even closer. Her thigh rests on top of mine now, and I wonder if she's noticed. I wonder if she's doing it on purpose, or just pulling toward me like a magnet to steel.

My water glass is sweating in my palm, and I set it on a coaster, not trusting myself to hold it steady anymore. Is this dorky talk about welding actually turning her on?

Is it turning *me* on?

*You're an idiot. A babbling, worthless, grease-monkey idiot.*

True, but I keep going. "Did you know that when you weld two dissimilar metals together, you have to be careful about coefficient thermal expansion at the joint of the two?"

I'm reciting from memory from the first welding guidebook I ever got my hands on. I was twelve, and someone had left it behind in a junk car at my dad's scrapyard. For years I thumbed those rust-spotted pages with a flashlight under the covers, badgering my old man to explain the jargon until I'd committed passages to memory and no longer needed to crack that duct-taped spine to remember the precise steps for welding nickel-based alloys to steel.

It's how I got where I am today, in a way.

I swallow hard and focus on Lisa. Her face is flushed, and she looks like she just bit into a juicy, ripe strawberry. Those green eyes flash with heat, and she lifts her fingers and touches the pearl necklace at her throat.

"Wow," she murmurs. "That does sound very hot."

I swear to God I didn't set out to turn her on with this. I was just trying to make her laugh, maybe build up her confidence a bit by telling her how hot she is.

I don't know if it's the multi-syllable words or the grease monkey thing that's getting to her. Does it matter?

Her bare knee rests on my leg, and I swear her skirt has hitched another three inches up that glorious, creamy thigh. I ache to touch it. It's like she reads my thoughts, shifting so her leg brushes the tips of my fingers.

I hesitate, then lift my hand. Her knee fits perfectly in my cupped palm, and I hold my breath, waiting for a reaction.

"More," Lisa whispers.

"More what?" I'm honestly not sure.

She licks her lips and darts a glance at my hand. When her eyes lift to mine again, I feel my cock throb.

"Tell me more about what's hot," she says. "The welding, I mean."

Good God, I can't believe my luck. Of all the dumbass lines I've used to seduce women, welding terminology never made the list. My heart hammers like a goddamn piston, and I scroll through my brain for more lingo. I lean closer, almost close enough to brush my lips against her ear.

"You want to hear about stick-shielded metal arc welding?" I murmur. "That's when you touch the electrode tip to the workpiece, then withdraw it really, really slowly."

"Oh," she murmurs, not quite a gasp and not quite a groan. "That sounds really hot."

"It is," I tell her. "Usually about sixty-five-hundred degrees Fahrenheit."

Jesus. I've been welding my whole adult life, and I never knew it could sound sexy. Lisa shifts again, and I don't know how it happens. One second she's squirming beside me, and the next second she's on my lap, lips parted, legs parted, her whole body pressed against mine.

Did I do that, or did she?

We're face-to-face now with Lisa on my lap, and she peers at me with uncertainty in her expression.

"Hello," I murmur.

It's a dumb thing to say with her lips scant inches from mine, begging to be kissed, but she smiles anyway. "Hello."

Her brow furrows with self-consciousness, but I don't give her time to go there. I close the distance between us, brushing my lips to hers as I slide my hands to her hips.

Then I'm kissing her hard and deep, groaning as she moves against me. Her body is like a coiled wire, tense with energy. I skim my hands up her sides, brushing the edges of her breasts to hear her whimper, then back down, curving over her hips and around. I clutch her ass and give a gentle squeeze.

"God, Dax." She breaks the kiss to groan, then arches against me. The movement hitches her skirt up around her hips, and I can feel the heat at her core pressing against the fly of my jeans.

"That's it," I whisper, conscious of the way she's grinding against me. I haven't been dry-humped since I was sixteen, and I can't believe how fucking good this feels. I wonder if I should slow things down, maybe be more tender with her. This can't be what she's used to.

But her words echo in my head.

*I want something different. Something that's the total opposite of what I'm used to.*

My hands move roughly up her sides, yanking her blouse

from her skirt. I stifle a growl as my palms graze bare skin. I've never felt anything this soft in my life, and I draw in a slow breath to clear my head. I kiss her again, needing to taste her. My hands keep moving, savoring her smooth flesh until my fingertips graze the lace at the edges of her breasts.

She gasps as I flick open her bra clasp with one hand, and I worry I've gone too far when she draws back.

Her lashes flutter as she blinks at me and tries to focus on my eyes. "I should take off my skirt so it doesn't wrinkle."

I skim my palms under her bra cups and test the weight of her breasts in my hands. She gives a soft moan, and I swear we both lose our train of thought.

My thumbs skim her nipples, and her eyes go wide again. I hold her gaze with mine, willing myself to form a coherent thought.

"Do you always take off your clothes for sex?" I ask.

She bites her lip. "I guess—I never thought about it."

"Then leave them on. *Everything.* Even your shoes."

Lisa blinks then glances down at her red-soled stilettos. Her fingers trace the pearl choker at her neck, and she nods slowly. "Yes," she whispers. "Clothes on. I want it like that."

"You want what?"

I'm pretty sure I know, but I want to hear her say it. Want her to be clear about what she's asking for, what she needs.

"I want you inside me." She blinks, startled by her own words. That makes two of us.

Then a slow smile tips the edges of her mouth, like a kid with her first taste of ice cream. She grabs hold of my waistband and leans close so her lips brush my earlobe. "Dax," she whispers like she's not sure how to say the words out loud. "Do me with my clothes on, please."

My dick lunges like it's trying to ram its way through my zipper, and it takes every ounce of self-control I own to give a measured response. "Yes, ma'am."

As Lisa plants slow kisses in a path behind my ear, I stroke my thumbs over her nipples. She shudders in my hands as I release those gorgeous tits and inch my hands down her stomach. I keep going, gliding up her skirt and dipping the tips of my fingers into her panties. They're a lacy wisp and probably expensive. I push the fabric aside and stroke inside her, groaning when I feel how wet she is.

"Christ," I growl against her mouth. "How did that happen?"

Her giggle turns to a groan as I graze her clit with my knuckle. "You," she gasps. "You did it to me."

I keep doing it, skimming the pad of my thumb over her clit while my index and middle finger move inside her. She responds by fucking my hand, slowly at first, then with increasing intensity.

Her hips move like they have a mind of their own. She tilts back, arching against me with her eyes closed. "Oh my God, that feels amazing."

My thumb strokes her clit again, and I'm rewarded with another moan. She's moving faster now, her body tense and coiled. We've hardly gotten started, and I can already tell she's close. Her eyes are closed, lips parted, her body tight like a bow.

"That's it," I murmur, kissing her throat. "Ride my hand. Show me how you like it."

She obeys, hips moving to a rhythm only she can hear. I can feel it, though, bubbling up inside her as she rocks and writhes and pants on my lap. "Oh God!"

The orgasm seems to surprise her, and her eyes snap open, blazing green and wild. I clamp one hand on her hip, driving my fingers into her as I strum her clit with my thumb. She pumps her hips, arching against me as she cries out and comes so hard that I'm trembling with it.

Then she collapses against my chest, panting like she just ran a mile. A few seconds pass before she opens her eyes and leans back to give me a sheepish look. "Sorry. Let me just grab some tissues so you can—"

"No." I slide my hand back, fingers slippery from being inside her. As she watches, I draw one finger into my mouth. Her lips part in shock as I suck deeply, tasting her sweetness.

"You're delicious," I tell her. "So fucking hot."

She stares at me like no man has ever said this to her before. How is that possible? She's squirming against me, moving like she's ready to go again.

"Please, Dax." She wriggles against me, fucking me through my clothes.

"Please what?"

Her lashes flutter, and I sense she's turning shy again. "You know what I need."

"I have a good idea," I murmur, nuzzling her throat so she's not forced to make eye contact. "But I want to hear you say it."

I catch her earlobe between my teeth and run my tongue over the pearl stud. I wonder what it would feel like to stroke her sweet little clit with my mouth, and suddenly I'm harder than I ever thought possible.

"Do you want me to fuck you, Lisa?"

She draws back, eyes wide with surprise. I sense she hasn't had a guy talk to her like this before. I also get the feeling she likes it. She nods, biting the edge of her lip.

"Yes," she whispers. "Yes, please."

"Please what?"

Her cheeks go pink, and she bites her lip harder. Okay, so she's not ready to talk dirty yet. That's cool with me. But something tells me she likes when I do it. I can tell by the way she's squirming against me, watching my mouth for the next filthy invitation.

"You want me to shove my cock in you?" I murmur. "Is that what you want?"

She nods so fast I think her head might fall off. "Yes. Oh God, yes."

Okay, then. No sense wasting any time.

I fumble into my back pocket, hoping to God I remembered to shove a condom in my wallet. I find the foil packet and yank it out, not caring that I just upended the contents of my billfold onto her spotless carpet.

Lisa reaches down between us, her fingers quick and clever on the button of my jeans. The denim is damp from her, and I half expect her to say something apologetic. Instead, she grabs my dick and pulls it out.

"Holy wow." She blinks up at me. "I—um. Wow. That's a little…uh…large."

I stifle the urge to snort-laugh. She did say she wanted something different from her usual fare, and apparently she's used to guys on the smaller end of the spectrum. "We can take it as slow as you want."

She looks down again, skimming the tip of my cock with her thumb. A bead glistens on the tip, and she uses it to glide her finger around the throbbing head "It's so…so…"

Big? Hard? I wait for one of the expected adjectives, one of the words she's heard in dirty movies and thinks she's supposed to say.

"Pretty."

Huh?

She gives an embarrassed smile. "Is that not what guys like to hear?"

"You called my dick *pretty*?"

"Well it is." She grips it in one hand, making my balls clench with need. She gives me a grin that shoots straight to my cock. "It's like the perfect color and shape and—"

"Are you planning to fuck it or decorate a room with it?"

She dissolves into giggles, making her tits jostle pleasantly beneath her silk blouse. "Oh my God! I'm an interior designer, and you just gave me the best idea for a room designed entirely in penis motif. There'd be penis-shaped throw pillows and a pink fainting couch in one corner with—"

"I'm going to come in your hand if you don't stop stroking me like that."

She stops moving her hand and grins. "Well. We wouldn't want that."

Before I can say anything, she grabs the condom and tears open the packet. She rolls it on with expert hands, and I'll admit I'm a little relieved she knows what she's doing.

She starts to slide off my lap. "Let me just take off these—"

"No." I grip her hips to hold her in place. Then I let go with one hand, and reach between us to shove aside the damp scrap of lace between her legs, baring her to me. Perfect pink lips glisten with wetness, and I ache with the urge to bury myself inside her.

I look up and meet her eyes again, wanting to be sure. "If this isn't what you want, tell me now."

She nods, then shifts her hips. Her hand is still on my cock, and I groan as she angles it toward her, trailing the tip through her wetness. "It's what I want."

Then she moves again, taking the first couple of inches inside. Her eyes widen, and I hold still. I could still stop now if I had to, and I brace for her to say it. But those aren't the words that fall from those perfect lips.

"Oh my God, you feel unreal."

I groan and skim my hands from her hips to her breasts. My thumbs tease her nipples, and I wait for her to make the next move. She's in control, and I sense that's what she needs right now.

"I want you to ride me," I tell her. "Slow and soft or hard and fast—you call the shots."

She nods, gaze locked with mine, almost like she's

mesmerized. Then she sinks down on me in one slick move.

"Oh my God."

She's the one who says that, but the words are in my head, too. Holy shit, she feels amazing.

She slides down again, breathless with pleasure as she begins to fuck me. Her hips move like there's someone else driving them, like she's been seized by some other force. She reaches behind me and grabs the back of the sofa, manicured claws sinking into the leather as she uses it for leverage.

"God, Dax." My name comes out of her mouth like a moan, and I can't believe this is the same woman I met at the bar.

She's thrusting and grinding and growling low in her throat. I start to reach between us to tickle her clit, but there's no need. She's already there.

"Oh. Oh Jesus, *yes*—"

She throws her head back and gives a primal scream I'm sure will have the neighbors summoning the cops. But there's no time for that now, as shapes start to shimmer behind my eyelids and I realize I'm right there with her.

"Christ," I groan as I let go.

We both come for what feels like forever, fucking and gasping and riding each other. When it's over, Lisa collapses against my chest again.

I stroke her back through the silk blouse. She's missing one of the buttons on her left sleeve, and I have no idea when that happened. Is she going to come down from the clouds and survey the scene, embarrassed? She'll take in her disheveled clothes, her mussed hair, the uneducated lug on her sofa and will devise the politest, most tasteful way to ask me to please get the hell out of her house.

I wait for the words to fall from those full lips as she leans back and looks me in the eye.

"Dax," she says. "I want you again."

# Chapter Five

## LISA

Dax gives me a startled look as he digests the words I've just spoken.

*I want you again.*

He stares at me for a few beats, seemingly at a loss for words. "I know you said some of this is new to you, but the male anatomy needs a little more time to—"

"I don't mean right this second," I say, waving aside the rest of his explanation. "I may be an uptight priss, but I'm not a virgin."

He raises an eyebrow at me, and I feel awkward straddling his lap like this. Then I replay what he just suggested, and the awkwardness ratchets up. "Wait, did you think I was a virgin because I'm not very good at—at—at all this?"

I wave my hand again, hoping the gesture is enough to sum up what just happened here.

Like it could ever be enough.

Dax grins and grabs my wrist, then plants a kiss on my

palm. He takes his time with it, sending a shiver that runs all the way from my hand to the point where our bodies are still joined. We should definitely get rid of the condom.

"Anyone ever accuse you of overthinking things?"

"Good Lord, yes," I say. "I never *stop* thinking."

He grins. "Smart girls are sexy as hell." He plants another kiss on my palm. "Relax, Lisa," he murmurs, and oddly enough, I do. "I didn't peg you as a virgin, a priss, or a woman who doesn't know how to fuck. You are none of those things."

The word *fuck* rattles through me more pleasantly than it should, and I realize these walls have heard the word more times in the last hour than they have the entire time I've lived here.

It also occurs to me that I really should get off Dax's lap. I try for solemn dignity, but feel ungainly as I swing one leg to the side and move back, smoothing my skirt down as I stand up. I do my best to straighten my blouse, making a vain attempt to tuck it back in before giving up and hurrying toward my bedroom.

"Give me just a minute to put myself back together," I call over my shoulder as I slam the door behind me before turning to lean against it.

What the hell just happened?

Before I can stop it, a grin spreads across my face as I remember *exactly* what just happened. Every last detail, from Dax's scruff against my throat to his hands on my ass to the thundering earthquake of orgasm. *Orgasms.*

Good Lord.

I can count on one hand the times Gary made me come more than once, and I'd have at least one finger left over. I use that finger now to make an obscene gesture in memory of that relationship and the asshole who left me standing there at the altar in my Vera Wang wedding gown and my Oscar de la Renta beaded peep-toes with—

*Knock it off,* I order myself. *You just had the best sex of your life with a guy who's the exact opposite of all that. Now get back out there and put the rest of the plan in action.*

The rest of the plan is fuzzy in the back of my head, but it's been percolating in my brain all evening. It begins to gel as I straighten my clothes, splash cool water on my face, and touch up my lip gloss.

When I return to the living room, Dax is standing in front of my stainless-steel wine chiller studying the bottles inside. It's an impressive collection, with reds and whites in separate, temperature-controlled compartments. It's one thing I fought for in my split with Gary, even though he kept the fancy house in the West Hills with the thousand-bottle underground wine cellar. This condo was mine to start with anyway, though I redecorated to remove any trace of Gary's four-year influence on my life. I wanted something *different.*

I stare at Dax now. He's certainly different.

"Hi," I say.

Dax smiles at me, and I try to come up with something clever to say to the man who just banged me senseless.

"There's an Evenstad Reserve from Domaine Serene in there," I say.

Christ. Can I be a bigger snob?

But Dax just smiles. "I've only had the 2013, but I hear the 2014 was much oakier."

I blink at him, dumbfounded. "It was sixty percent French Oak instead of fifty-seven. You know wine?"

The utter shock must be obvious on my face, and Dax straightens his shoulders.

He takes a step back from the wine chiller and holds my gaze, unblinking. "Sorry to kill your fantasy about having sex with a knuckle-dragging Neanderthal who can't tell a decanter from a champagne flute and spells Cabernet with a K."

"I—I—I never thought—"

"Yeah you did." He gives me a small smile, and there's no ice in his voice, but still. I can tell I hit a sore spot. I'm not sure what that's about.

"Sorry," I tell him, not sure what else to say.

"Not a problem," he says. "It's good to know wine for business, plus I happen to enjoy it."

I glance away, embarrassed by my own assumptions. By the fact that I've judged him without really knowing him. It's not the first time someone's caught me in the act of being pretentious and judgmental, but it's the first time it's really stung. I start to swing my gaze back to Dax when it snags on his wallet upended on the floor. I stare for a few beats, pretty sure I'm seeing things.

"Holy shit." I blink at the jet-black credit card fringed with silver, then look at Dax. "Who are you?"

He follows my gaze toward the couch, then gives a small, dry laugh. Taking his time, he ambles over and picks up his wallet. Then he walks back toward me, shoving cards and ID back in his wallet, but not that one. The black card he holds up, giving me a clearer view of it. I've never seen one up close.

"This? Is this what you mean?"

I nod, too surprised to play dumb. "I just—that's an Amex Centurion Card. Isn't it?"

He nods and shoves it back in his wallet. But I've already seen enough to know it's the real deal. "Not to hang up on this or anything," I say slowly, "but doesn't that card have like a seventy-five hundred-dollar initiation fee and another twenty-five hundred in annual membership charges?"

He looks at me oddly. "Are you a banker?"

"No, but I almost married a stockbroker whose life's ambition was to have one of those cards."

Dax shrugs, not seeming too concerned. "I know you

wanted to fuck a penniless dirtbag from the wrong side of the tracks," he says. "If it makes you feel any better, that's really where I come from." He clears his throat. "And I really do know how to weld."

*And how to fuck*, my brain adds, and I wonder when my subconscious started talking like a sailor.

I also wonder why he's belaboring his point about my assumptions. "Look, I'll admit I might have judged the book by the cover," I say slowly. "But you have to admit you did the same thing with me."

I have him there. I can tell by the way his eyes narrow just a little, and I remember the conversation in the bar about grudge fucks. There's a story behind that, but now's not the time to push for it.

There's something else I want.

I smooth my hands down my skirt, doing my best to regain my composure. "Let's start again," I say. "Thank you for the best sex of my life."

He blinks, then starts to laugh so hard he grips the edge of the wine chiller to keep from doubling over.

"God, Lisa," he says. "I've gotta hand it to you. You never say exactly what I expect you to."

I'm not sure if that's a compliment or insult, but it seems like a good sign he's laughing.

"Right," I say, wishing this were a little less awkward. "I wanted to propose something to you. Not marriage," I clarify when I see him blanch. "Or a relationship of any kind, I promise. This is strictly a no-strings-attached kind of thing."

His eyes glint with intrigue, and I take a step closer, thinking this conversation would be easier if we each had a glass of that damn Pinot Noir in hand. As I reach for the handle of the wine chiller, Dax catches my hand and lifts it to his mouth.

"Hey," he murmurs. "You're right—that was fucking

amazing."

I flush and try to mask how much that means to me. I'm used to people praising me for my skill at floral arranging or canapés or a hundred other things like that.

But not for crazyhawt monkey sex. He really looks like he means it.

I clear my throat and draw my hand back, grateful for the rush of cool air that hits me as I open the wine chiller. I take out the bottle and hold it up, pleased when he nods approval.

"Tell me where the glasses are," he offers.

I direct him toward the hutch then busy myself opening the bottle and pouring it into a decanter. The whole thing feels so domestic. How do normal women conduct themselves after a casual hookup? I'll have to ask my sister, Cassie.

When we're finally seated back on the couch, I wait until he's had his first sip to get down to business. "You enjoyed the sex?"

He sputters into his wineglass, then gives me a bemused nod. "Yes. Very much. Are we going to debrief now? Make a spreadsheet to highlight our favorite moves?"

I have to admit, I'd like to know. But I tamp back my curiosity in favor of getting to the point. "Here's the thing," I begin. "I slept with you because it seemed like the exact opposite of what my normal instincts would be. The opposite kind of guy, the opposite circumstances, the opposite type of sex."

"Type of sex?"

"Type," I repeat, not sure how much to spell out. "Lotus position on the couch with all our clothes still on, as opposed to—I don't know—missionary position under the covers with a tasteful negligee cast aside at precisely the right moment."

"Lotus position?" Dax grins. "Did you just turn our hot, spontaneous animal sex into something that sounds like a floral arrangement?"

"Exactly!" I smack the couch with the back of my hand, startling us both. He probably thinks I'm nuts, but he doesn't move away.

"Look, the sex was amazing," I say.

"You mentioned that."

"I'd like to try a test," I tell him. "Not an 'are we compatible' quiz from Cosmo or anything like that," I clarify when I see his brow crease. "A test of my own instincts."

"How do you mean?" He sounds dubious, but also interested. I take that as a good sign.

"Well, since doing the opposite of my instincts went so well this time, what if I tried it for a whole month? Like every time I have a decision to make, I do whatever the opposite of that would be."

"Are we talking strictly sex, here?"

I shake my head as I feel heat creep into my cheeks. "Some sex, yes. But not just that."

"Give me an example," he says. "A non-sex one."

"I don't know." I fumble around in my brain for something that doesn't involve sex, but it's tough to do with Dax sitting beside me looking like sin on a stick. "Say my normal breakfast is a whole-wheat bagel with low-fat, artisan Neuchâtel cheese and a smattering of lox with homemade capers and a side of organic berries. Instead of that, I might have…I don't know—"

"Chocolate chip pancakes?" Dax offers.

"Yes!"

I can't read anything from his expression. Does he think I'm crazy, or is he seriously considering this? He takes his time responding. "Are you asking me to be your tour guide to chocolate chip pancakes?"

I nod, thinking it sounds weirder when he puts it that way. I hold my breath, wondering if I've just ruined a good thing. If I've just made an ass of myself or offended him or screwed this up in some other typically-Lisa fashion.

"Look, I know I'm asking you for a favor here, but maybe there's something I can barter with." I flutter my lashes, hoping he gets the message, but guessing he thinks I have dust in my eye. "I'm sure there's something else I can offer."

I graze his knee with my hand, hoping to drive the point home. Dax stares at it a moment, then looks at me. "Oh, you've got plenty to offer."

I wait for him to spell it out. To tell me what might make my proposal appealing for him. If I go through with The Test, I want us both to benefit. I want Dax to tell me what would make it worthwhile for him.

He lifts a hand and tucks a strand of hair behind my ear. I shiver from the warmth of his touch. From the fact that I want more of it. *A lot* more.

"I accept."

I blink. "Really?"

"Don't sound so surprised. Today was fun. And if you're after someone to suggest biker bars and best practices for keg-stands, I think I can help you out."

I start to ask what's in it for him, but I stop myself. That's hardly a good negotiating tactic.

But Dax reads my mind anyway. "Let's just say I enjoy the pleasure of your company."

Well, okay then.

The word *pleasure* ricochets through my mind, making me shiver.

It's then that I pledge to have as much sex as possible with Dax Kensington before The Test is through. It's the least I can do for the sake of science, right?

# Chapter Six

## DAX

Twenty-four hours later, I'm sitting in my La-Z-Boy with ESPN on the TV and a bag of barbecue chips in my lap, wondering what the hell just happened.

Not with the football game, though God knows I've been too distracted to pay much attention to the score.

The second Lisa marched out of her bedroom yesterday with her perfectly retouched hair and an "I have a plan" look on her freshly made up face, I knew she was up to something.

I just didn't know *something* would be a proposal to fuck each other silly while I introduce her to—well, whatever the opposite of "the finer things in life" would be. Slumming it?

She judged right that I know what that is. But she judged wrong that it's all I know. Seeing her expression when she realized I'm loaded was priceless.

It's also the reason I agreed to The Test.

The chance to grudge fuck a hoity princess from the other side of the tracks? Sign me up.

Okay, fine. She's not like other socialites I've known, especially my ex. I can admit that now. The hair color looked similar at first, but Lisa turned out to be nothing like I thought. She's more fun than I expected. Not the polished kind of sexy, but the sweet, funny, smart-as-hell, blow-my-fucking-mind kind of sexy. Is it so surprising I'd want that again?

I'm saved from answering my own douchey, defensive question when the phone rings.

*Lisa Michaels*, the readout says, and I'm annoyed by how happy that makes me.

"Yo," I answer, getting into the spirit of The Test. That's the opposite of how people in her circle would normally answer the phone, right?

"Um, yo?" Lisa's greeting comes out sounding more like a question, but then she laughs. "My normal instinct would be to wait for a guy to call me first after a date, so according to the rules of The Test, I'm calling you first."

"Very nice," I say, more delighted than I ought to be. "You get a gold star and a cupcake."

She giggles, and I realize just how much I love that sound. "A cupcake," she repeats. "That sounds nice. I could use one after the day I had."

"Want to tell me about it?"

"No, I just called to see if you might be free next Saturday for—"

"You should, then."

"What?"

"Talk about your day," I say. "If your instinct says not to, then you should."

She's quiet, probably wondering what the hell this has to do with our sex game. So am I.

Or maybe I'm not. Maybe I enjoy the soft lilt of her voice on the phone. Maybe I want to hear about her day. Is that so weird?

Lisa clears her throat. "I don't like to complain about work to anyone."

"All the more reason you should," I tell her. "Maybe it'll feel better to not bottle things up inside."

"Well," she starts slowly, hesitating. "First I had a client throw a royal fit because the drapes I ordered for her are more cornflower than cerulean."

"They both sound delicious."

She laughs. "Then I got a call from a couple I've been working with for six months to redesign their penthouse apartment," she continues. "Apparently, they're divorcing and want to cancel the job."

"Maybe they'll move into separate homes and you'll get to decorate both."

"That is a good thought." There's a clink of a glass, and I wonder if she's sipping the rest of the wine from yesterday. I wish I were there with her to enjoy it, to rub her feet as she tells me about her day.

*Wait. What the hell is going on?*

"Anyway," she says, "After that meeting, I took my sister-in-law to lunch, and even though we made it perfectly clear we needed a gluten-free meal, they brought out salads with croutons."

Something about her words annoys me. Makes me want to lash out about first-world problems and made-up dietary drama and—

"Isn't the gluten-free trend a little last year?" It's a lame jab, but it's the best I've got.

"Excuse me?"

There's an unexpected sharpness in her voice, and I can't figure out why she's getting so uptight. Kaitlyn got like that, too, always villainizing some new food group. First it was carbs, then dairy, then gluten. Never for any medical reason, mind you. She was just following the trend.

"Look," I tell Lisa, determined to do what she's asked me. To break her out of that mold. "How about we go out for a nice, greasy pizza, and—"

"For your information," Lisa snaps, "Celiac disease is common in people with Down Syndrome. If Junie eats gluten, she's sick for days."

It takes me a second to process what she's just said—and the fact that I'm a total fucking dickhead. I swallow hard, trying to regroup. "You have a sister with Down Syndrome?"

"Sister-in-*law*," she corrects. "Well, technically, Cassie and Simon aren't getting married for a few more months, but I think of his sister like one of my own. Anyway, we sent the salad back after she had one bite, but she had a stomachache when I dropped her off, and the whole thing made me feel awful."

I sit there in silence for a moment, wondering if I've misjudged Lisa. If I've written her off as an uptight princess who has to have everything her way. I start to apologize, but she's already talking again.

"Anyway, I think I'll call the spa down the street to see if I can get in for a massage tomorrow," she says. "That seems like a good way to decompress."

"No," I tell her. "That's what you'd normally do, right?"

"Right," she says slowly. "You're not going to ban spa days, are you?"

"Maybe not ban," I tell her. "But if you're looking to feel better, I have an idea for how to accomplish that."

The words come out more suggestive than I intended, and I know she's taken them that way when she gives a funny little purr.

"Well," she says. "I like the sound of that."

My dick throbs at the thought of where she just went, but I order myself to stay cool. "I'll call you at eight tomorrow morning with directions," I tell her. "Dress like you're going to get dirty."

Then I hang up, wondering what the hell I've gotten myself into.

# Chapter Seven

"You want me to scrub him *where*?"

I blink at the friendly attendant who wears a perky ponytail and a rubber apron identical to the one draping my torso. She's holding a mop-colored terrier and giving me an encouraging look.

"Part of the intake process for grooming new rescue dogs is making sure they're thoroughly clean," she says with a lot more cheer than seems appropriate from someone uttering that combination of words. "All you need to do is lift the tail and—"

"Didn't Doctor Swanson say she wanted to check out some of the smaller guys?" Dax steps between us and touches my hip with one hand. The smile he's giving the woman makes her quiver like a saucer of Jell-O, and I can't say I blame her.

He has that effect on me, too.

"Oh." Jell-O girl beams up at Dax. "Good point. And I suppose it *is* Lisa's first day volunteering at Helping Paws."

"Exactly," Dax agrees. "We want to keep her coming, don't we?"

His voice is liquid chocolate, and I shiver when he says that last part. He slides a glance at me, and I try to pretend I wasn't just having dirty thoughts about him in the grooming suite at the dog rescue facility where he volunteers every weekend.

According to Dax, today's experience is the *opposite* of a spa day, which makes it perfect for The Test.

It also makes for a very smelly experience. Wet and filthy and very, very stinky. I'm doing my best to be a good sport, but taking grooming tips from Jell-O Girl might be my tipping point.

"So how about Lisa and I finish up in here," Dax says to Jell-O girl, and I snap my attention to him. "And we can let Doc Swanson take care of the other details."

His hand is still touching my hip, and I'm amused to realize how much I like it there. And how much Jell-O girl does not. She shoots me a smile buttered with faux cheer and turns her attention back to Dax.

"The vet just finished up with that Chihuahua, so I'll just grab Scooter here and run him next door," Jell-O girl says, still beaming at Dax like he gave her a pair of diamond studs and a G-spot orgasm.

"That sounds fantastic," Dax says, and it takes me a second to remember they're not talking about orgasms.

Jell-O girl scoops up the terrier and trots out of the room. I turn to Dax and blow a damn tendril of hair off my face. "I have to admit, this is not what I expected when you mentioned doggy style."

He grins and jabs a thumb over his shoulder toward the Pekingese mix I just finished blow-drying. "I'm positive that dog has never had so much style in her life," he says. "I don't know how you got that little pink bow to look that good."

"I've had a lot of practice with specialty knots."

"Me, too," he says, and eyes me in a way that has me thinking about that time my book club read *50 Shades*. I'll admit, I was scandalized.

Now, I'm more...*curious.*

"You doing okay?" Dax asks.

I adjust my ponytail and try to look like a woman who wasn't just thinking about bondage. "I'm good." I sniff the sleeve of my sweater and wonder how long I'm going to smell like wet dog. I'm pretty sure it's permeated my pores. "Thanks for rescuing me there."

"You're welcome," he says like a perfect gentleman. A tattoo-covered gentleman who's been wrestling unruly canines all morning, including two big Rottweilers who weigh more than I do. Is it wrong that I find it kind of hot?

"You're doing a great job, by the way," he tells me.

He sounds surprised by that. He's not the only one. I'll admit I was taken aback when Dax explained that today's addition to The Test involved bathing and grooming a batch of dogs rescued from a hoarding situation in Gresham.

But the instant he placed a scared, matted Pomeranian in my arms and ordered me to make her pretty, I got it. I may not be a dog person, but spa days are my jam.

"Those little pom-pom things on the poodle were a nice touch," Dax says. "Stuff like that helps them get adopted."

"She really was a sweetheart," I tell him. "Did you notice how she perked right up after her bath? It's like she knew she looked beautiful."

"I noticed. And I'm amazed that Labrador let you paint her toenails."

I laugh and adjust my damp ponytail again. "She seemed mellow enough to try it. I could never pull it off with any of those terriers."

He smiles and looks me up and down, then shakes his

head. "I still can't believe you wore high heels and pearls to wash dogs."

"Well, you didn't tell me we were washing dogs," I point out. "You just told me I should dress to get dirty."

"And to you that says 'put on seven-hundred-dollar jeans' instead of 'where's my dominatrix costume?'"

"They were a gift," I fire back. His mention of a dominatrix costume has my cheeks flaming, so I choose to nitpick the rest of his comment instead. "How do you know how much Roberto Cavalli jeans cost, anyway?"

The expression he gives me is stony, and I'm not sure what triggered it. "Let's just say I have experience removing them," he says after a long pause.

I stare back at him, not sure if he's trying to make me uncomfortable or if he's compensating for his own discomfort.

"Not that it's any of your business, but the jeans were a present from Gary four weeks after he ditched me at the altar and then had a change of heart," I tell him. "He showed up with a dozen roses, a bottle of Veuve Cliquot, and the jeans he knew I'd always wanted."

"And you were all too happy to take them?"

I roll my eyes at him. "I chased him down the walkway and threw the roses at him," I snap. "Then I put on the damn jeans, called my sisters, and spent the evening drinking the champagne and toasting to my good fortune at not marrying the asshole."

Dax stares at me for a few beats. "You surprise me sometimes."

"I surprise myself sometimes."

He studies me a moment longer, then nods at the bank of dog kennels lining the wall. "For what it's worth, you've done great here today. With the dogs, I mean. I figured you'd last ten minutes, tops."

"Well, you figured wrong."

"I did," he says. "I may have misjudged you."

His words warm me as much as those icy-blue eyes, so I decide not to mention the fact that I *did* consider fleeing after ten minutes.

"I like being helpful," I admit, which is mostly why I stayed. "With the dogs, I mean. Everyone deserves a chance to look and feel their best, and if it helps them find homes, then I've done something right."

"That's the spirit." He turns and starts toward the bank of kennels. "Come on. Let's keep scrubbing."

I step up beside him, remembering what Jell-O girl told me earlier. "Some of these littler ones are afraid of men," I remind him. "I can grab her."

I unlatch the door of an upper kennel and greet a curly black terrier with fearful eyes. "Come on, sweetie," I coax, edging my hand into the kennel. "We're going to make you soft and pretty and clean smelling so you'll find your new home."

The dog gives me a dubious tail wag and shoots a nervous glance at the hulking man beside me. Dax steps back, giving me space to work. "Don't you worry about him," I murmur to the dog. "He might look scary, but he's really quite sweet."

Dax snorts behind me, making the dog jump and give a halfhearted snarl. "Now, now," I soothe. "You don't really mean that. You're just playing tough because you're scared. I know all about it."

I keep my voice low, the words spilling out of me secondary to the soothing tone that's worked wonders on skittish canines all morning. Slowly, the dog's ears perk up, and her skinny black tail gives a tentative wag.

"There you go, babycakes. Is that your name? Babycakes?"

"It's a boy," Dax points out. "How about Axel or Deathmetal?"

"Deathmetal?" I roll my eyes at Dax, but the dog gives a soft yip and dances forward. He leans down and licks my hand, wiggling in earnest now.

I seize the opportunity to scoop my hands under the wiry little body, and the dog doesn't resist. "Oh my. Yes, you are a boy, aren't you?"

"For another day or so, anyway," Dax say. "There's a strict Helping Paws policy on spaying and neutering every pet that comes through the doors."

Deathmetal pricks his ears and gives another soft yip, and I stroke my hand over his ears. "Don't listen to him," I soothe. "I'm sure he's just teasing you. And even if he's not, I promise all the lady dogs will appreciate a man who has contraception covered."

The dog licks my hand again as I carry him toward the bank of tubs on the opposite wall. Dax moves beside me, rubber apron straining over his huge chest. "You've seriously never had a dog before?" he asks.

"Nope." I take my time lowering Deathmetal into the elevated, stainless steel tub, scratching his ears so he stays relaxed. "Our parents never allowed it. Said they were messy and uncouth."

"You've spent your life avoiding all things messy and uncouth?"

"Something like that."

He says nothing in response, so I'm not sure why I find myself blushing. I turn my face to the side, concentrating on adjusting the taps to get the water just right. Beside me, he squeezes dog shampoo into his oversize palm. After doing this all morning, we've got our system down. Still, his presence affects me, the way he stands close enough that I can feel the heat from his body.

"There you go, baby," I say to the dog as Dax begins massaging suds into the curly black fur. The dog stiffens at first, but I keep a gentle hold on him. Soon, Deathmetal relaxes, giving in to the soft pressure of Dax's hands engulfing his small frame.

"There's a spot right here," I murmur, directing Dax's hand to a patch of burr-matted fur under the dog's chin. His fingers brush mine as he begins to work the knot with gentle, powerful movements.

"That's a good pup." He leans closer, his breath grazing my ear as he reaches across me for the detangling cream. His bicep brushes the edge of my breast, and I remind myself this is the least-sexy activity imaginable.

"Feels good, huh?" he murmurs as he works the detangler into the matted fur.

I nod on Deathmetal's behalf as the little dog thumps his tail in agreement. I scoot the wiry body to the side to give Dax better access to the pup's soft underbelly. He reaches across me again, this time grabbing for the handheld nozzle. I lean back against his chest, telling myself I'm only making room for him to position the spray just right. That I'm not just a hussy who can't get enough physical contact with this man.

He aims the nozzle at Deathmetal, splashing blissfully warm water over the backs of my hands. "You like that, hmm?"

Deathmetal gives a satisfied sigh, and I swallow hard and focus on turning the dog around, angling the little wet body up so Dax can rinse him off.

"Almost done, sweetie." My voice cracks a little, and I wonder if Dax has any idea how much his nearness is affecting me. "You're such a good, good puppy. Just a few more seconds."

Dax leans past me again to set the hose aside, and I shiver, curious if he's doing this on purpose.

But no, he's just hanging up the hose, going through the motions of dog grooming. He grabs a fluffy gray towel from a pile beside the tub and turns to me with a conspiratorial grin that makes my toes curl. "Want to see a trick for getting a dog to shake off so you don't have to do so much toweling?"

"You just now thought of this?" I spit out a hunk of my hair, determined to cover my discombobulation with a hoity air. "Instead of twenty dogs ago, maybe?"

He grins. "Something reminded me just now."

Then he leans past me, bending low so one meaty bicep brushes my hand. He's eye level with Deathmetal now, and he uses one massive finger to gently lift the edge of the dog's ear.

"Just like this," Dax says. Then he purses his lips and blows into the dog's ear. Deathmetal twitches into a full-body shake that sends tepid water spattering against the sides of the tub and the front of my apron.

Dax grins and stands up again. "Good boy!"

I laugh because it's funny, but also to cover the fact that I'm seriously smitten with this version of Dax. The gentle giant and clever animal handler. The guy whose hands are the size of small skillets and whose fingerprints I can still feel all over my body.

I scoop the dog up and hand him to Dax so he can bundle him into the gray towel. Then he hands Deathmetal back to me, and I set to work rubbing down the wiry little body.

"You're right, this is much better," I say. "He's already mostly dry."

"Sorry I didn't remember earlier," Dax says. "I was distracted."

The way he's watching me makes me forget I'm soggy and bedraggled and smelling like wet dog. There's admiration there, surprise, even.

And also desire. I don't think I'm reading it wrong, but I concentrate hard on toweling off the dog so my knees don't buckle. Seriously, how is this getting to me? I don't understand at all.

"Dax," I murmur, needing to break the tension. "I want you to know that—"

"Okie dokie!" Jell-O girl bursts through the door and bustles over to us, her perky ponytail swaying from side to side. "Looks like I timed that out just right."

"Perfect," I murmur, still dizzy from Dax's closeness.

"The second crew just got here for cleanup, so you two are free to go now that this last little guy is done."

"Last one?" I turn back to the stacks of cages, amazed to realize they're empty. "Wow. We've been busy."

"Great work, you two," she says. "Will we see you again next week?"

She's talking to Dax, but he looks at me. "I'll be here for sure. And maybe now that Lisa's gotten a taste of it, she'll keep coming back for more."

"That would be awesome!" Jell-O girl says with a forced chipper tone that says it's as awesome as herpes. I can't blame her for wanting Dax to herself.

But right now, so do I.

I wait until Jell-O girl has bustled out of the room with Deathmetal before turning back to Dax.

"I think I'm ready for a shower," I say.

His eyes flash with interest as he steps closer, then slips a hand under my super-sexy rubber apron to skim my hip. "You need some help with that?" he murmurs. "I've been told I'm quite proficient with the shampoo."

My stomach flips, and I meet his flirtatious tone with my own. "I promise to shake if you blow in my ear." Okay, that sounded sexier in my mind.

But he grins back anyway and leans close to graze his lips over my earlobe. His breath is warm against my neck, and the way he's touching my hip leaves no doubt he wants me as much as I want him.

"Let's get out of here," he says.

# Chapter Eight

## Dax

Nothing today is going quite like I thought it would.

First, Lisa agreed to forego her spa day to wash thirty smelly, homeless dogs. Color me impressed.

Is it wrong that I half expected her to walk out the door the second she got a whiff of wet canine? But she hung in there like a champ, putting those immaculately manicured nails to good use scrubbing flea dip into matted fur and soothing scared pups with murmured assurances that had me edging closer just to hear her voice.

It's the first time I ever got a hard-on at the damn dog shelter.

But my plan to bring her back to my place for a steam shower and a soak in the Jacuzzi went sideways when every damn drawbridge in the city was up for an incoming Coast Guard vessel. The Hawthorne, the Broadway, the Burnside, even the Morrison were all conspiring to keep me from getting laid. When the bridges are up in Portland, there's no getting from the industrial east side to the residential west side of the river. In other words, we were trapped in the ghetto.

Luckily, I had a backup plan.

"Faster!" Lisa urges, wrapping her legs tighter around me as her claws sink into the tops of my pecs.

At least, I think that's what she said. It's tough to hear with the helmet muffling my ears and the scream of my motorcycle's engine covering her voice.

I rev the throttle in response, and Lisa's grip tightens around my chest.

"We're almost there." I take a turn a bit faster than normal, loving the way she laughs like this is a carnival ride.

When she told me she'd never been on a motorcycle before, I had to remedy that. Blame it on The Test, blame it on my desire to feel her body pressed against mine. Either way, it got us here on the back of my Ducati.

I pull the bike into the covered parking area in front of my workshop. Being on the wrong side of the tracks—or bridge, as it were—has an upside. This industrial part of Portland isn't pretty, but it's a prime spot for manufacturing the steel-walled bottles that made me stupid rich.

It also has a shower, which is why we're here now. If we can't make it to either of our homes, this will have to do.

I park the bike and tug off my helmet, pausing to tuck it in the locked gearbox on the back. Then I then turn to grab Lisa by the hips. "So this is where the magic happens," she says.

"Yep. Headquarters for CoolTanks double steel-walled reusable water bottles."

"It's nice," she says, though *nice* is hardly the word to describe this rundown warehouse on the fringe of Portland's inner-eastside. It's butt-ugly, but it gets the job done.

I set Lisa on firm ground, then fumble the straps on her helmet. Tucking it under my arm, I grab her hand and start tugging her toward the shop. "Right this way."

I sound like a fucking tour guide, or maybe like a sixteen-year-old boy who's hoping to get laid for the first time. But since Lisa devised The Test to get no-strings sex and a glimpse of life's seedier side, maybe that's not the worst thing.

I unlock the rolling steel door and shove it back. The smell of metal shavings and heated plastic rushes toward us, a scent as familiar and comforting as my morning bacon.

But not to Lisa, who hesitates in the doorway and lets go of my hand. She takes a few steps forward, and I brace myself for a snide comment about the dust and dirt and disarray.

"Wow."

I'm instantly on alert for judgment. "It ain't the Ritz Carlton," I mutter, determined to beat her to the punch.

She tosses an eye roll over her shoulder, then ignores me and moves toward the far corner of the room. It's then that I realize what's captured her attention. A funny lump clogs up my throat.

"It's amazing." Lisa reaches up to brush a hand over the sculpture. "Did you make this?"

"Yeah." I nod, equal parts embarrassed and defensive. "I—uh—usually keep it covered. Sheet must have fallen off."

"Wow," she says again, circling the sculpture like an art critic. "I love mixed metal, and this piece is especially fantastic."

"Thanks." My chest swells, but I keep my pride in check as I watch her hand trace the lines of the sculpture. It's a little abstract, but still obvious it's a wolf. At least to me, since no one else has seen it.

"Wolves are such majestic creatures," Lisa murmurs, answering the question I'm too chickenshit to ask. "And you've captured it so exquisitely. All the sharp angles and powerful curves. It's really beautiful."

"Thank you." My throat is tight, and I'm not sure why it

feels so strange to have Lisa here marveling over my work.

"What made you choose a wolf?"

I take my time answering, choosing my words carefully. "School mascot."

"High school or college?"

The words spark something unpleasant in the core of my chest. "High school. Not all of us had the money or the smarts for college."

Lisa ignores my sharp tone, but studies me. She's watching my face like she knows there's more to the wolf story than I'm saying. Like she knows the reason I'm being kind of an asshole.

"You're really talented."

"Thank you." I swallow back the lump in my throat and shrug. "I'm not really an artsy kinda guy. It's just a little side project I've been playing with."

I don't know why I'm trying to downplay this, but the intense way Lisa's studying my face says she's onto me. That she knows there's a story here.

But she doesn't push. "Sometimes," she says slowly, "those little deviations from the norm have a way of changing the way you look at things. At yourself."

I nod, not sure I want to get into this. Not sure how to feel at all. Part of me is guarded, but part of me wants to hear what she means.

"It was like that for me and decorating," she continues. "I thought I just wanted to play with throw pillows and buy expensive furniture with other people's money, but it turned out I had a knack for design. For determining how things function within a certain space." She smiles a little sheepishly. "I guess I like when I can surprise myself that way."

"Yeah. I can see that." I don't know why I feel vulnerable and edgy. I shrug and nudge the sculpture with my toe. "It's been fun, but I'll probably junk it when I'm done."

"Don't!" She says it like I've just threatened to toss a puppy off a bridge. "You have to keep it. It's beautiful. Raw, but full of movement and energy." She gives me a smile that's almost shy. "I hope you do more of it."

Her words leave me feeling awkward and exposed, so I grab her hand and nod toward the far corner of the space. "Come on. Let's get cleaned up."

She laughs and lets me pull her toward the corner bathroom. I say a prayer the housecleaning crew has come through sometime in the last month, but even if they haven't, I know it won't be pretty.

I'm not wrong.

"Oh," Lisa says. "This is—quaint."

"Is quaint another way to say disgusting as hell?"

The space is barely larger than a coat closet, with a sink, a toilet, and a standup shower. It's clean and pretty new, since I had everything installed six months ago when I doubled my workforce and implemented a program encouraging employees to bike to work. A shower comes in handy for that.

And for post-dog washing hookups. At least that was the hope. Now, I'm not so sure.

"It's not disgusting," Lisa says. "It's just—small."

A flicker of annoyance flares in my chest, which is stupid. It's an employee bathroom at a metal shop, not a luxury spa.

But something about the judgment puts me on edge. It's a painful contrast to the hard-on throbbing in my pants at the sight of Lisa in her damp pink T-shirt. I'm deciding which response to ignore when she turns back to me with nipples clearly visible through the thin cotton. Lust surges through me again as she smiles.

"God, I'm dying to get out of those clothes."

I swallow hard. "No objection from me."

"Are we—uh—showering separately, or together?"

I love that she's unsure. That she didn't come here with

an agenda for some elaborate shower seduction.

"Are you normally one for showering solo or with someone?"

She laughs. "I don't like to share water. We've also never seen each other naked before, so—"

She trails off, and I realize she's right. And the flush in her cheeks makes it clear she's nervous about that.

"Hey," I say, stepping closer and lowering my voice. "I'll never push you to do anything sexually that you don't want to do. Test or no Test."

"Thank you." She bites her lip. "I guess I do get a little prudish about nudity. I suppose if I'm being true to The Test, I should work on that?"

She won't get any objection from me there, but I want this to be her call. I settle for nodding sagely, waiting for her to decide.

The instant she does, there's a mischievous flicker in her eyes. Then she grabs the hem of her T-shirt and yanks it over her head.

"Guh," I manage, to stunned to form words as I stand there gawking like a redneck at a tractor pull. I don't know if I'm more impressed by her pink lace bra, by what's inside it, or the fact that she had the cojones to bare it all.

Either way, there's no way in hell I'm going to leave her standing there topless by herself. I yank off my T-shirt as well, though what I really want to do is reach for her. Or unzip my fly. My dick strains painfully at the front of my jeans, struggling to escape.

Lisa stares at my chest, eyes sweeping over my shoulders and down my abs. Her throat moves as she swallows and returns her gaze to mine. "God, you're big."

"Maybe it's relative," I tease. "It's a pretty small bathroom."

She smiles back and runs her palms down her thighs. "I

suppose I should take off another article of clothing."

"Totally up to you," I say, even though everything inside me is screaming for her to just get naked already.

"Hmm... Do shoes count?"

I hesitate. "If that's what you want to take off next."

She looks at me from beneath her lashes and lowers her voice. "What do *you* want me to take off?"

Wait, what? Is this a trick question?

Or is Lisa toying with something else here? Like maybe she gets off on being told what to do?

I hesitate, then take a risk. "Your toes are hot and all," I manage. "But I'd rather see your tits."

It's a jarring word, and I wait for her to slap me. I'll apologize if I'm wrong, but I don't think I am. Lisa Michaels likes dirty talk. She just never knew it before.

Her eyes flash with desire, and I watch the emotion play out on her face. Lust. Uncertainty. Longing. No one's ever talked to her like this before, and she's not sure she should like it.

Seeming to decide something, she lifts her hand and toys with the front clasp on her bra. I can't tell if it's an unconscious gesture or if she knows what she's doing. Either way, I sense she wants me to call the shots. To tell her what to do next.

"Take it off," I command. "I want to see you."

She hesitates only a second, then flicks the clasp open. She turns her head so her ponytail slides over one shoulder, covering her right breast. The other she hides with her elbow as she drops the bra on the counter and stands looking at me.

Her shyness undoes me, but so do her next words.

"Your turn."

I grin and pretend to ponder. "Hmm, what else can I show you?" Holy hell, I'm dying to get my pants off. Having a beautiful, topless woman in my bathroom is giving me the mother of all hard-ons.

I move a hand to my fly and watch Lisa's eyes drop. Does she realize she just licked her lips while staring at my crotch?

"Should I take off my pants?" I ask.

Lisa doesn't take her eyes off my junk, but she nods like I've just asked if she wants a scoop of double-fudge ice cream. "Okay," she murmurs.

I make it a two-for-one deal, shoving off my jeans and boxer briefs in one motion. I kick my shoes off in the process, then stand there wearing nothing at all.

There's a moment where I realize this is the first time I've been naked with this woman. Sure, I've been inside her, but I've never stood in front of her like a goddamn nude statue.

"Sweet baby Jesus," Lisa breathes. She lifts her gaze and meets my eyes again. "You look really good naked."

The earnestness in her words is unbearably sweet, but also hot as fuck. How does she do that?

"Care to join me?" I murmur.

Her cheeks pinken just a little, and I'm charmed by her self-consciousness. We've fucked like animals in her living room, but seeing each other naked for the first time is different. It's a big deal, especially to her.

I take a step forward, ready to back off at the slightest sign she's not ready. Lisa studies me, then drops her arms to her sides. Her throat moves as she swallows, and I'm aching to plant a kiss on that sweet spot at the base of her neck.

"I want to touch you," I tell her. "Do you want that?"

She nods and tips her chin up, baring her throat to me.

"Yes," she murmurs. "Touch me, Dax."

I don't need to be asked twice.

My hands slide up to cup her breasts, teasing, stroking. She gives a soft little moan and melts into my arms. I bend down to take her nipple in my mouth, and she cries out and clutches my hair.

"You like that?" I murmur against the soft underside.

"You taste so fucking good."

Her body arches in my hands, and I can tell my words have gotten to her. That she likes what I'm saying and the way I say it.

I move my mouth to the other nipple, sucking the soft peak into my mouth. My thumb strokes her other nipple, gliding over the wetness I've left there. She groans and grips my hair.

"Say that again," she whispers. "I like when you talk."

Talk *dirty* is what she's saying, or at least I think so. I give it another shot. "You have the most perfect tits," I murmur against one of them. "Burying my face in them is like a fucking dream."

She groans and throws her head back, lost in my words and in what I'm doing with my mouth. I can tell she's giving in to the sensations, letting herself go as I slide my hand into the front of her jeans and dip my finger into—

"Wait!"

I jerk back so fast I give myself whiplash.

"We should shower first," she says. There's a bashfulness in her expression that amuses me. "I'm all sweaty from working all day and—"

"I kind of like you sweaty." I grin, hoping she knows it's true. "But we can definitely shower if you want."

She bites her lip, and I wonder if this is part of The Test. Is sweaty, un-showered sex not part of her repertoire? Then again, maybe I owe it to her to make sure I'm squeaky clean, too.

I let go of her and reach into the shower stall, I grab hold of the tap and twist. And twist. And twist. And twist. And—

"What the hell?" I step into the shower and frown up at the nozzle. "Is the water out or something?"

Lisa reaches for the taps on the sink. "Looks like it," she says. "Did you forget to pay your water bill?"

The question makes me bristle. I know she's joking, or maybe she's not. She can't possibly know I spent my whole damn childhood having our water and electricity and everything else shut off for unpaid bills.

I swallow hard and order myself not to let dark thoughts ruin the moment. I jerk the shower handle again. Dammit. "I'll get dressed," I mutter. "The main line is outside on the street."

I start to reach for my pants, but Lisa grabs my wrist. "Wait."

I stop, pants dangling limply from my hand, even as my dick still throbs like an over-eager python.

"What?" I ask.

Lisa licks her lips. "You know what I'd normally do right now?"

"Run screaming from the building?"

She giggles, then nods. "Maybe not that dramatic. But I'd probably get all prissy and insist we're not engaging in any sort of sexytimes until we're both freshly washed."

"I see," I tell her, a little weirded out that she used the words "sexytimes" and "freshly washed." But I can see wheels cranking in her head, and I like where they're going.

"I guess the opposite of that would be—"

She doesn't finish the sentence. Not with words, anyway. Instead, she gives me a wicked grin, then turns and grabs a towel off the wall. I'm speechless as she drops it onto the shower floor, then meets my eyes and grins wider. "Here's the new plan."

*Holy shit.*

I stare in stunned silence as she drops to her knees on the towel. Then she grabs the base of my cock and smiles up at me. "I've always kind of wanted to do it like this."

Her tongue flicks out and grazes the tip of my cock, and I practically lose my mind. I have to grab the soap dish to stay upright as Lisa forms an *O* with her mouth and slowly sucks me in.

*Jesus fucking Christ.*

Her mouth is the softest thing I've ever felt in my life, warm and wet and so sweet that I might actually pass out. She takes me in deep, giving a low little moan as she sucks me in.

When she draws back, her green eyes flash as she tosses her ponytail over one shoulder. "Oh, I definitely think I'm going to like this."

# Chapter Nine

## LISA

I've given blowjobs before, okay?

Tidy, post-shower fellatio with my hair pulled back and the perfect synchronicity of suction and tongue action. Minimal slobber, thank you very much.

But this is different. My own private test, if you will.

I suck Dax in as deeply as I can, seeing how far I can go, pushing my limits. I'd forgotten how huge he is, and there's a moment of panic where I think I might gag and embarrass myself.

But I don't gag. Instead, I relax. And in relaxing, I realize I like this. I love it, actually.

I love the way he fills my mouth, threading his fingers through my hair as I move slowly up and down his shaft, taking my time to explore every ridge with the flat of my tongue. He gasps when I graze a spot near the tip, so I focus more attention there, licking and sucking and making soft little circles. There's slobber on my chin, but I don't even care.

How nuts is that?

His fingers tighten in my hair, and he groans. "Lisa," he gasps. "You're so fucking good at that."

His words send a rattle of pleasure through me, and I love this version of myself. The one who can kneel on an unfamiliar shower floor and suck a guy off like a goddamn porn star. It's empowering. It's liberating. It's—

"Delicious," I say, easing back to wipe a corner of my mouth with the back of my hand. A flutter of embarrassment wiggles in my chest, and I wonder if that's really what the porn star version of myself would say. But it's true and it feels right in the moment, so I say it again. "I like the way your cock tastes."

The words sound weird and stilted, and for a moment I'm afraid my first attempt at dirty talk has fallen flat. But Dax stares at me with undisguised pleasure and tightens his grip in my hair. "God, you're nothing like I expected."

I'm not sure if that's a compliment or not, but I'll take it as one. Truth be told, I'm surprising myself, too.

I'm also surprised to realize I like it when Dax talks dirty. I love it, actually. I love when he tells me what to do, and I really love hearing how something feels to him.

"Can I ask you for something?" The words spill from my mouth before I have a chance to think them through.

Dax grins. "You're gripping my dick right now. You can ask me for a fucking pony if you want."

I laugh as those words ripple through me. Not *pony*—I mean *dick* and *fucking*. Guys don't talk to me like this, or at least not the ones I've dated.

I want more.

And while pre-Test Lisa would count on passive-aggressive cues or subtle moans to get what she wants, this one is going to ask for it.

"Talk dirty to me, Dax," I say. "Tell me what you want

me to do to you."

He stares at me a moment, then nods. "I want you to suck my dick so hard your cheeks hurt," he says. "See how much you can take."

I groan and shift on my knees, conscious of the pressure between my legs. His words have me dripping with need, and I wonder if he knows it.

"Okay," I say, and lick my lips.

Then I lick him again, starting slowly with the head. I swirl my tongue around him, then move down the shaft, sucking him deeper and deeper until I feel him touch the back of my throat. I see stars, but they're not stars of discomfort.

They're the good kind of stars.

His hands are back in my hair, rougher this time. He must sense that's what I want. "That's it, baby," he groans. "You suck me so good."

*Yes!*

I've been praised for many skills in my life—the perfect soufflé, my knowledge of wine pairings, my knack for holiday decor.

But being praised for BJ skills sends a rush of pleasure through me that's like nothing I've felt before. It's exhilarating.

So are the throaty moans Dax is making, an audible sign of how good this feels to him. How good I'm making him feel.

"That's it, baby," he murmurs. "Lick the tip just like that. God, you're so fucking good."

I grip the base of him, loving how much control it gives me. I lick him like a perfect scoop of cherry gelato and wait for my next command.

"Fuck," he groans, which isn't exactly a request. Or maybe it is.

"You like that?" I slip my hand between his legs, cupping him in my palm. "You like it when I touch you there?"

I can't bring myself to say *testicles* or *balls* or whatever a real dirty talking woman might say, but I can see my words are getting to him anyway. Or maybe it's what I'm doing with my fingers.

"Yeah," he groans. "Use your nails just like that. *Fuck*."

I suck him in deep again, drawing him back into my throat. His fingers tighten in my hair as I start to slide back, ready to do it again.

"Stop," he groans.

I pull back, fighting a wave of disappointment. "Did I do something wrong?"

He shakes his head and gives a soft little laugh. "You're doing everything right. That's the problem. I'm not gonna last if you don't stop."

"Oh. *Oh*." My face heats up, and I think about telling him not to stop. That I want to get him off like this.

But that's not the only thing I want.

He grabs my hand and hefts me to my feet, reading my mind. "Take off your jeans," he commands.

His words send a surge of lust through me, but also a twitch of nerves. I take a deep breath and peel off the jeans, shucking my shoes and panties, too. As I straighten up, I realize it's the first time he's seeing me naked. I fight the urge to cover myself. Part of me wants to put an arm across my muffin top. To press my palms against my breasts so he doesn't notice they're not very big.

But I do none of that. I square my shoulders and throw my ponytail over one shoulder, determined not to be *that* Lisa. The one who arranges her body at the most artistic angle like she's posing for a boudoir selfie.

Dax is silent as he takes me in. I hold my breath, not sure how to read the stoniness of his expression. The tic pulsing beside his right eye.

It's the heat in his eyes that gives him away, followed by a slow blink like he's trying to clear his vision. He rubs a hand over his jaw, the stubble making a scritch-scritch sound that sends pleasant goose bumps rippling up my arms.

"God, you're beautiful." His voice is thick and gravelly. "So fucking stunning."

It's the sexiest I've ever felt.

"Jesus, look at you." He takes a step forward, and turns me around so I'm facing the mirror. He's right, I do look pretty good. Not perfect—not by any stretch of the imagination—but my whole body radiates desire like it's been painted with candlelight.

I watch myself in the mirror as he skims a hand over my breasts, bringing me back to the present. I'm aching for him to bury himself inside me. I don't even want the shower I came here for. I just need Dax. *Now.*

"What do you want?"

I think about what I want, what I need, what instinct is telling me I should do. They're all different things, and the options whirl in my brain in a pink-tinged mist of lust and desire and longing.

But there's one thing I'm sure about.

"I need you inside me, now." I lick my lips, then add as an afterthought, "Please."

Dax smiles, then tips me forward against the counter. I grip the edge of the sink, eager for what comes next.

"I want you to watch yourself," he says. "I want you to see how beautiful you are."

I meet my own gaze in the mirror, then his. His eyes hold mine as he strokes a hand over my ass, caressing it like a cashmere sweater. One hand glides forward to cup my breast, and my next breath catches in my throat. My face in the mirror is like no version of Lisa I've ever seen. She's wild and wanton and flushed with pleasure.

I think I like her.

His cock bumps into the ridge above my tailbone, and I

press back against it without thinking.

"You want that, baby?" he asks.

I nod and meet his eyes in the mirror. "Yes," I whisper. "Please, Dax."

*Please fuck me* is what I'm thinking, even though I don't say it. He hears the words anyway, and his eyes flash with hunger. It's like telepathic dirty talk.

There's a crinkle of cellophane behind me, and though I can't see his hands in the mirror, I'm relieved he has a condom. As mind-numbed as I am with lust, I might have forgotten.

"Watch yourself in the mirror," Dax urges. "I want us both to see me sliding into you."

I do as he says, pulse throbbing in my ears. I can't see everything, not from this angle, but I can see enough. I can see the hard, latex-sheathed length of him vanishing slowly into me.

But, oh God, I can feel it. I'm dizzy with pleasure, aching from the delicious intrusion. He's hard and huge and oh-my-god, he's bigger than I remember. I cry out as he fills me completely, and he goes still.

"You good?"

I nod and meet his eyes in the mirror. "I'm better than good." I bite my lip. "Talk dirty to me again?"

He laughs, but not like he's making fun of me. Crinkles of pleasure frame his eyes, and he smiles at me in the mirror.

"Oh!" I gasp.

"You like that?" he growls, and I grip the counter tighter. "You like it when I'm balls-deep in that tight little pussy?"

His words yank the breath from my lungs, and it's all I can do to nod. Nod and grip the counter and pray like mad he keeps doing what he's doing. My God, I've spent a lifetime cringing when I heard words like these in movies. Why are they the hottest things on earth when they're tripping from

Dax's tongue?

"Dax, please," I manage to gasp.

"You want it harder?"

How does he know that? It's like he's reading my mind, which scares the hell out of me and thrills me all at once. "Yes," I whisper, and Dax obliges, turning my whisper into another groan of pleasure.

There's an audible smack of flesh against flesh, and I clutch the counter harder. Years ago, I had one of those Clapper things to turn off my bedside lamp, and I think of how the goddamn lights would be flashing like a strobe right now.

"What's making you giggle?" Dax growls. It's not a mad growl, though, and he smiles as I meet his eyes in the mirror.

"This," I gasp as he slams into me again. "You. All of it—I just—"

I stop myself there, too giddy to trust myself with words. My brain has switched off, overpowered by lust and pleasure and whatever voodoo magic Dax is working right now.

I giggle at the thought of Dax fucking me in a magician's cape, earning another snort from him.

"You're lucky I have a healthy self-esteem," he says. "Otherwise, I might wonder why you keep laughing."

"I can't turn my brain off," I admit. "I keep having silly thoughts, but ohmygod—" I suck in a breath as he drives in deep and hits something really good. "Don't stop!" I squeak out.

He grins at me in the mirror. "Let's see if we can't shut off your brain, hmm?"

He drives in hard again, gripping my hips, and I wonder if I'll have bruises tomorrow. I hope I will. I want physical proof of the best sex I've ever had in my life.

"I want you to come for me, baby," Dax murmurs. "You think you can do that?"

I nod, even though I'm doubtful. The man knows female anatomy, clearly, so he must know that in this position, the friction isn't happening in quite the right spot.

"Touch yourself," he murmurs.

I blink at him in the mirror. "What?"

"You heard me." Dax drives into me again. "Rub your clit, just like you would if you were alone in bed thinking of me fucking you like this."

I swallow hard, turned on by the words even as they terrify me. Sure, I've touched myself plenty when I'm alone. I've even had boyfriends stroke me there when the situation called for it. But touching myself in front of someone else?

*Remember The Test…*

"Okay," I gasp, and draw my fingers up between my legs.

The effect is electric. I gasp as my index and middle finger glide slick over the sensitive bud. Missiles of pleasure launch through me, and I buck against Dax as he pounds into me again.

"Oh!" I cry out, closing my eyes to absorb the pleasure.

*Holy hell, this feels amazing.*

"That's it, baby," he urges. "Open your eyes and watch yourself."

I do as he says and see myself with tousled hair, bee-stung lips, and a hulking, sexy-as-hell tattooed god pounding me from behind.

*Who is that woman in the mirror?*

My face is scant inches from the glass, fogging it with sharp breaths of pleasure. I look blissed out. I look sexy. I look like a woman who's about to come her brains out.

"Dax—" My voice is unfamiliar and primal.

"That's it," he growls.

His words, and one more stroke, are all it takes. Then he's driving into me as the orgasm grabs hold of my whole body and throws me into a spinning centrifuge of pleasure.

Sensation pulses through me with each thrust, with every slick stroke from the pads of my fingers. My breasts smoosh into the counter, giving me the delicious contrast of cool porcelain and raw heat and explosions of pleasure everywhere around me.

Dax slams into me again, and somewhere in the back of my brain, I realize he's coming, too. The spasms inside me give way to more, and I realize my own body is responding, yanking me back onto the rollercoaster of pleasure.

Holy shit, is this what they mean by multiple orgasms?

We're both breathless by the time the sensation stops. I lie there spread across the counter, this panting, grinning, unrecognizable version of me.

Dax meets my eyes in the mirror and smiles. "You okay?"

He doesn't wait for me to answer. Just pulls me up against him where I bury my face against his chest and nod and grin and giggle without meaning to.

"I'm amazing," I breathe. "Was it good for you, too?" I do a mental face-palm at the sound of those words. "That was dorky, wasn't it?"

Dax just shakes his head and strokes a hand down my back. "That was fucking phenomenal."

I smile. "Agreed."

He turns me so I'm leaning against the shower wall. It's a good thing, too, since my legs were about to give out. "Was that a little outside your comfort zone?" he asks. "The dirty talk, touching yourself—all of that?"

I nod as heat creeps into my cheeks. "A little, but isn't that the point?"

"Definitely," he says. "But I hope you know you can tell me if you don't want to do something."

"I know."

I may not know Dax well, but I can trust him with this. My body, my safety, my heart—

No. Not my heart. That's not what this is about.

I smile and try to think of something witty to say. Something breezy and flirtatious so he understands we're on the same page with this casual sex thing.

I'm still thinking when there's a gurgle from above, followed by a blast of icy water.

"Aaaagh!" I shriek as Dax spins me around so he's shielding me with his body. We're both laughing as he fumbles for the taps, twisting off the icy blast of water. "Fuck!" he gasps as he cranks the knob, tattooed forearms wet and flexing.

When he turns to face me, we're both dripping and laughing like idiots. "Well," he says. "Looks like the water's working."

I dissolve into giggles again, certain I haven't laughed so hard in years.

Certain that the potent stew of emotion simmering in my gut is way more intense than I'd bargained for. I expected fondness, not passion. Pleasure, not joyful delirium. Insert tab B into slot A and all that jazz, but this—this—whatever it is with Dax… It's not like anything I've known before.

Dammit.

Dax grins, and I wonder if he's read my mind. "Ready for that shower now?"

I shoot a nervous glance at the showerhead. "Does it have a setting besides frigid?"

"Let's find out."

I take a step back, and Dax turns the knobs again. Water burbles from the showerhead with a little less intensity than before, and he takes a few seconds to adjust the taps. "There," he says, running a hand under the water. "That should do it."

He holds out his slippery hand, and I take it, letting him pull me under the spray with him. Warm water sluices down my body, and I sigh as he glides his hands down my arms and back up again, palms fitting perfectly over the curves of my shoulders.

"That feels good," I murmur.

I'm not sure if I'm talking about the water or his touch. Steam billows around us, and I glance down at my pink-tipped toes looking small and fragile with Dax's feet on either side of them. I tip my face up again and let the warm droplets patter across my forehead.

Dax smiles and brushes a damp hank of hair off my forehead. "You okay with sharing the shower, or would you rather take turns?"

Something about experiencing this with Dax seems right. It's not just The Test, either. It's a closeness that has nothing to do with my experiment and everything to do with being utterly overwhelmed by what just happened between us.

"I'm not used to sharing," I admit. "But I want to with you."

God, that sounded cheesy. But Dax doesn't laugh.

"Turn around," he says.

I must look startled, because he smiles and shakes his head. "Not for that," he says. "Turn around, and I'll wash your hair for you."

"What?"

He grins and grabs a green bottle from the rack hanging around the showerhead. "That's assuming you can handle generic Dollar Store shampoo touching your perfect hair."

There's a challenge in his voice, but also something soothing, warm and gentle like bathwater. I pivot on the slippery shower floor, conscious of Dax moving behind me. There's a click of the bottle top opening, followed by a billow of cedar-scented steam filling the small space.

"That's it," he murmurs as his hands close over my scalp. His fingertips start to move, massaging soft, languid circles along my skull. He lifts my hair off my shoulders and works his way down, massive fingertips kneading the spot where my head meets the top of my neck. I groan as his thumbs work that spot for several heavenly moments, loosening something inside me.

My shoulders go limp with bliss.

"There you go," he murmurs. "That's the spot."

God, it's like a massage and a hair appointment all in one, with the bonus of a hot, naked tattooed guy in charge of it all. I didn't know that was a thing.

I close my eyes as he works his way down, gentle as he lathers the shampoo into a fragrant cloud around my head. He takes his time, careful to swipe the suds from my brow. He's murmuring something low and soothing, but I can't make out the words. It could be a lullaby or a recitation from a welding manual for all I know. Whatever it is, it sounds as good as this feels.

I lean back against his chest, letting Dax tip me back to rinse the froth from my hair. The shower nozzle must be handheld, because he's guiding the spray along the back of my head. My eyes are still closed, but his fingertips feel like a dream threading through my hair, kneading my scalp until I'm on the brink of purring like a housecat.

"That feels delicious," I murmur.

"That's the idea."

I sigh and let him keep massaging. The suds are probably long gone, but he hasn't stopped touching me. Hasn't stopped threading his fingers through my hair, skimming his palm over my shoulder to brush away bubbles.

What is it about this that's so much more intimate than what we were doing fifteen minutes ago?

Bent over the bathroom counter, I was sure I'd reached maximum pleasure. I thought that was the best I could possibly feel.

I was wrong. So damn wrong about everything.

Why can't I stop smiling?

# Chapter Ten

## DAX

"Okay, we're coming up on another corner," I shout. "Hold on tight!"

There's a hoot of delight from behind me, and I glance across the parking lot to see Lisa standing on the curb, beaming in a yellow sundress. At her request, I've offered to fulfill her sister-in-law's lifelong dream of riding a motorcycle.

Junie is the first person I've known with Down Syndrome, and I'll admit I was nervous at first. I didn't know what to say or how to act.

But five seconds in Junie's company made it clear why Lisa adores her. It's not a pitying "let's be nice to the developmentally disabled person" kind of affection, either. Junie's zest for life is contagious, and her enthusiasm for the motorcycle ride has me grinning like an overgrown kid on a Ducati. I've had plenty of women on the back of my bike, but none have made me laugh like Junie.

"Woohoo!" she shouts. "Hey, Lisa! Take a picture,

okay?"

Lisa obeys, snapping furiously. I take another lap through the parking lot of the warehouse, slowing down so Lisa can get a good shot of her sister-in-law.

"Here we are," I say as I ease to a stop near the mailboxes. I park the bike and help Junie off as Lisa hustles over to assist with the helmet.

"How'd you like it?" I ask.

"It was awesome!" Junie beams and gives me a hug so fierce, I stagger with the force of it. I hug back and smile at Lisa over Junie's shoulder.

"Think you're ready to join a motorcycle gang now?" I ask.

Junie steps back and seems to mull it over, then shakes her head. "Maybe not yet. You should probably take me for more rides so I get practice."

"I like how you think."

Lisa smiles and hands me the helmet, then turns back to Junie. "You ready for our lunch date?"

"Yeah. Can I wash my hands first?"

"Sure thing," Lisa says. "I'll show you where the bathroom is."

As Lisa leads her to it, I try not to think illicit thoughts about the last time I was in that bathroom with Lisa. It's been almost a week, and I haven't stopped thinking about it. Haven't stopped feeling my fingers in her hair or remembering the way water sluiced off her bare shoulders as I washed her back.

See? It's not just about the sex.

*The hell it isn't. And it damn sure needs to stay that way.*

Lisa emerges from the workshop with sunlight sparking off her blond hair and breasts rounding out the front of that yellow dress, and it's all I can do not to drool as she approaches.

"When can I see you next?" I blurt before I have a chance to think of something cooler to say.

She smiles and tucks her hair behind one ear, giving me a view of a tender swath of neck I'd like to be kissing. "I wasn't sure we were doing that," she says.

"Doing what?"

"I don't know." She shrugs and glances away, her gaze flitting over the bike, the mailboxes—anything but me. "Making dates. Acting like we're in a relationship or something. We both said we didn't want that."

I can't tell if it's a statement or a question, but I nod anyway. "Of course."

"So, we're still on the same page?"

"Definitely."

"Excellent."

She sounds so relieved that it's hard not to take it personally. But her words underscore exactly what we both want, so there's no fucking reason it should bother me. "The no strings thing is great," I assure her, or maybe I'm assuring myself. "Glad it's working out."

And it's true. Come on, the last thing I need is to date someone seriously. Especially with someone whose idea of a date involves a six-course meal or tickets to some Shakespeare play or—

"The damn opera."

"What?" I yank my attention back to Lisa, surprised to see she's pulled out her phone and is studying the screen with a frown.

"The opera," she mutters as she shoves the phone back in her purse. "I forgot I have to go to this fancy opera thing tomorrow night. I don't suppose you'd want to go with me?"

"To the opera?"

She nods and laughs. "The fact that you just said 'opera' the same way you'd say 'circumcision' is enough of an answer.

It's okay; I don't want to go either."

"Why are you?"

She shrugs and fingers the pearl necklace at her throat, making my mouth water unexpectedly. "A client gave me the tickets. It's one of those things I have to do every now and then to rub shoulders with the wealthy, influential crowd. The kind of people who need an interior designer."

I nod, even though the words send a ripple of unease through me. Social climbing was one of Kaitlyn's favorite forms of exercise.

"You sure you don't want to go?" Lisa asks. "I could use a hot guy on my arm."

Her words are teasing, and I should be flattered. Besides, who am I to get annoyed that she wants to use me when this whole damn arrangement is about using each other?

Still, I can't help feeling like the grungy kid from the wrong side of the tracks whose high school prom date laughed when he showed up in a thrift store suit. I didn't have enough money to rent a tux or to buy her a damn wrist corsage.

It's one of many reasons I hate dressy events.

I clear my throat now and focus on Lisa's invitation. "Do you even like the opera?"

"Not especially."

"How many times have you been?"

She considers that for a moment. "In the last year? Five, maybe six times. I used to have a season pass when—" She stops there, but I can hear the end of the sentence in my head.

*When I was with Gary.*

I'm really starting to hate Gary.

"So right now, are your instincts telling you to go to the opera?" I ask her. "Are you saying to yourself, 'I really *should* do that,' or do you genuinely want to be there?"

She sighs. "I suppose it's more of an obligation. For my career, for my clients—"

"Will your clients fire you if you don't show?"

"Maybe." She shrugs and gives me a sheepish shrug. "Probably not. Honestly, I'm not even sure they'll be there tonight."

"What would the opposite be?" I ask. "The opposite of a ritzy night at the opera?"

Lisa's brow furrows, and she scuffs her sandal on the curb. "I have no idea." She gives a self-deprecating little laugh. "Maybe it's my lack of imagination that's been holding me back all this time."

"I don't know," I say, leaning close enough to brush my lips against her earlobe. "You didn't lack imagination in my bathroom the other day."

I edge back in time to see her blush bright pink from her cheeks to her forearms. She's picturing it in her mind, and I'm glad. Visions of our bathroom hookup have been playing in an endless loop in my brain since last Saturday.

"The opposite of getting dressed up and going to the opera." I pretend to mull it over, even though I know exactly what that would look like. "Going to a biker bar wearing a leather miniskirt and a Mötley Crüe T-shirt with no bra. Eating hot wings, drinking beer, and maybe playing a round of darts."

"Wow." Lisa blinks at me. "That's pretty specific."

I grin back at her, noticing she didn't say no. "That's my specialty. When it comes to The Test, it's good to have friends in low places."

"I guess that's what I signed on for." I can't tell from her tone if she's intrigued or leery. Maybe a bit of both.

"Are you game?" I ask.

There's a challenge in my voice, and I wonder if I'm expecting her to say no. If part of me wants her to confirm she's not willing to try something new, to set foot on the seedier side of town.

After a few seconds of hesitation, Lisa shrugs and gives a small smile. "Sure. Why not?"

Huh. I'll admit the words surprise me, as does the pang of elation rippling through my gut.

"Besides," Lisa continues, unaware of the emotional yo-yo that's bonking around in my brain. "The opera tickets are good through the end of winter. I can hit next month's show as soon as The Test is over in a few weeks."

And just like that, I'm annoyed again. It's stupid, really. This is what we agreed, isn't it? A temporary fling, a temporary experiment. Nothing more than that.

So why do the words feel thick as I force them out of my throat? "Absolutely," I tell her. "You can do it next month when your life is back to normal."

"Thanks, Dax," Lisa says as Junie steps out of the workshop and heads toward us with her face lit by a smile. "You know how to show a girl a good time."

The words echo in my head, hollow and taunting.

*A good time. A dumb lug who's good for a fuck. That's all you'll ever be.*

I grit my teeth and remind myself that's what I agreed to. Nothing more, nothing less.

• • •

"Nice shirt."

It's the first time in my life I've uttered this phase while admiring an actual shirt and not its contents.

*Okay, I'm also admiring the contents.*

Lisa plucks the fabric away from her chest and studies her handiwork with a critical eye. "You can't tell where I singed the edge with the iron?"

I shake my head and skim a finger over the iron-on Mötley Crüe patch she's affixed to a navy silk polo shirt. "You covered it up with the fancy stitching around the edges," I tell her. "Bonus points for the umlauts over the O and the U."

"Thank you." She smooths her hands down her skirt, which I've already been informed is Rebecca Taylor luxe faux leather in cognac with an angled, knee-length ruffle designed to ripple when you walk.

It's part of their new spring line.

Lisa catches me staring and gives me a fretful look. "Is this not what you had in mind?"

It isn't. Not even close. I pictured a ripped black muscle tee and a miniskirt so short it could double as a placemat. Lisa looks like something out of a *Better Homes and Gardens* spread.

But it's fucking perfect.

"You look great," I tell her. "The hottest chick I've ever seen wearing a silk Mötley Crüe polo shirt with a long leather skirt and shoes that cost more than my car."

Lisa glances down at her dazzly Gucci gladiator stilettos and shrugs. "It's not every night a girl gets taken to a biker bar."

"True enough."

We both turn to survey the biker bar, which seems oddly smoky. Oregon banned smoking in bars almost a decade ago, but the perma-haze that fills the space looks like a mob of Hell's Angels lit the building on fire.

As we step through the doorway, Lisa clutches my arm. Part of me expects her recoil with distaste at the peanut shells on the floor, the sweaty smell emanating from the leather-clad bikers at the end of the bar, and the two drunk guys shoving each other by the pool table. It's probably all unpleasant to a woman wearing three-hundred-dollar lingerie under her leather skirt.

Yes, I do know about La Perla. And I can tell she didn't follow my "no bra" edict, which makes me more eager to get her out of it at some point.

I jump when Lisa yanks my arm and points. "Look. They have karaoke!"

I follow the direction she's gesturing and frown. This isn't the biker bar I know and love. "That's new," I mutter. "They don't usually do karaoke here."

One of the leather-clad dudes gives me an irritated glance, and I lift a hand to let him know it's all cool. That I'm not some hipster tourist scoping out dive bars from a guidebook. He surveys my tattoos, my ratty jeans and motorcycle jacket, and goes back to nursing his beer.

My date might be a stunning peacock in a cluster of crows, but I look like a guy who belongs here.

I step closer to Lisa and lower my voice. "You do karaoke?"

"God, no." She gives a mock shudder and smiles. "My sister is great at it, so I've gone out with her a few times. I love watching."

I file that information away in the back of my head, wondering which of her sisters is the singer. "Why don't you grab a seat over there?" I point to a booth to the left of the karaoke setup. "I'll grab us some beers and meet you in a second."

"Okay." She sashays away, and I watch her go. She's right—the damn skirt ruffle does ripple. And even though it comes down past her knees, it's somehow infinitely hotter than the black leather miniskirt I pictured in my head.

Go figure.

I glance around and realize I'm not the only one in the bar checking her out. Several guys glance up from their beers to watch her hips sway, and I want to grab every last one of them by the shirt and order them to look away.

*Mine,* I telegraph to all of them.

That's true for now, anyway.

I sigh and step up to the bar to order a couple of Budweisers and a plate of wings. Then I grab the beers and make my way across the room to where Lisa sits with her legs crossed primly and her hands folded on the table. She's glancing around, studying the scene, and I wonder what it looks like through her eyes. Is she disgusted? Intrigued? A little of both?

I set a beer on the table in front of her and take a seat on the opposite side of the booth. Lisa smiles, then stands up and moves over to sit on the bench seat beside me.

"What's up?" I ask, though I don't mind a bit. In fact, I love feeling her thigh snugged up against mine and her hair brushing my arm.

"The Test," she says. "I've always sat across from my dates in booths. Never beside. Figured I'd try it like this for a change."

"Works for me."

That's the understatement of the year. I gulp my beer, trying to keep my mind off the fact that the side of her breast just grazed my arm. I wonder if she's doing it on purpose and decide not. That isn't who Lisa is.

Then again, maybe she's as eager to have me touching her as I am. I take another swig of beer, skimming my bicep across her breast on the way up.

Lisa shivers and gives a soft little sigh.

*Damn.*

"So, Dax," she says. "Tell me about yourself."

I'm instantly on guard. "What do you want to know?"

"Well, you've met my sisters and my sister-in-law," she says. "You know all about my split from my ex and my dog-free childhood, while I know almost nothing about you."

It's true, and it's by design. But that's not going to cut it with Lisa. I can tell from the look she's giving me, like this is a job interview and she just asked me to describe my career history in detail.

I take a deep breath and spin my pint glass on the table. "I have a brother in prison and a sister who passed away."

"Oh." I glance up to see sympathy flooding her eyes. She moves her hand to rest it on my arm. "I'm so sorry."

She doesn't ask what happened, and I don't mean to tell her. But something about the warmth of her fingers on my forearm has me spilling out the details. "My sister, Dana, died of a heroin overdose at nineteen," I say. "And my brother is doing six years for second-degree armed robbery."

I'm not sure if I say this for shock value or for sympathy, but that's not what she gives me. There's compassion in her eyes, sure, but no trace of pity. No trace of scorn or shame. "God, Dax. I'm so sorry. Your poor parents."

I stare at my beer, considering how much to tell her. "Our dad died three years ago, and our mom left when we were little, so it's really just my brother and me. Paul—that's my brother—he's at the State Pen in Salem."

"Do you see him much?"

I nod and take a sip of beer. "Yeah. Once a week I drive over there for visiting hours. He's three years in, and there's a chance he'll get an early parole next spring. Good behavior and all."

"I hope he does. I hope it works out for you.

"Me, too." My chest feels tight, and so does the nod I give her. "We'll see."

Her hand is warm on my arm, and her eyes are kind. "How do you think you avoided it?" she asks. "Falling into crime or drugs or whatever. What kept you off that path?"

I study her face and see she's genuinely curious. Not judgmental, not pitying, just interested in my life choices.

I take a sip of beer and consider the question. "I guess I always wanted something better for myself. I saw the decisions my dad made, my sister made, my brother—and then I thought, 'how can I avoid fucking up like that? How can I make totally different choices?'"

Lisa nods and looks down into her beer. "It's like The Test."

"What?"

"You made a decision to do the exact opposite," she says. "To choose different things for yourself when you realized the other choices were dead ends."

I stare at her, dumbfounded. I'd never thought of it like that before. "I guess so."

"Is that why you agreed to help me?"

I shake my head, still amazed she made that connection. Is there something to it? Is it true that Lisa and I have that in common?

I pick up my beer and take a sip, too rattled to respond right away. This whole conversation is way too intense, and I feel like I'm sitting naked on this cracked vinyl bench. I have to defuse it. To keep her from getting any closer.

"Maybe I just wanted to sleep with you."

Lisa blinks at my dickhead answer, but doesn't flinch. There's nothing in her eyes that says my words bothered her.

"Mission accomplished." She lifts her glass in a mock toast. "You have officially crossed crazyhawt sex off my bucket list. And dirty talk, a fling with a stranger, and pretty much everything else required to complete my sexual education. Nicely done."

*Done?* Wait, no.

"Let's not go patting ourselves on the back just yet," I tell her. "There's still plenty of ground to cover."

"What do you mean?"

"We've barely even scraped the surface of your sexual reeducation."

She lifts an eyebrow at me, but there's intrigue glinting in her eyes. "Such as?"

"Oh, plenty of sex positions. Tons of things I'm sure you've never tried."

She tips her head to one side, blond hair skimming the M on her chest. "Like what?"

"Take the Screaming Weasel, for instance."

"The Screaming Weasel?"

"Yeah. Like, are we going to need to order extra duct tape and tomato paste for that, or do you already have a good supply?"

She's studying me like she can't tell if I'm yanking her chain, so I keep going. "Or maybe the Upside-down Radish," I say. "That's more of an advanced move, but I think you're ready for it. You aren't claustrophobic, are you?"

A smile flickers over her face, and she sips her beer with a knowing look. "That should be fine," she says slowly. "But I'm really more interested in the Paisley Parasol. Do you think my shellfish allergy will be a problem?"

I snort and run a finger through the ring of moisture from my beer glass. "Nah, we'll be good as long as the gas mask is nice and snug." I sip my beer and fight to keep a straight face. "Of course, we could always start with the Blue Rhino Tusk."

"That does sound intriguing."

I pretend to study her, though I'm mostly just after an excuse to admire the way her silk shirt hugs her curves. Mötley Crüe really should consider marketing silk polo shirts.

"Yeah, I think you've got the upper body strength for that one," I tell her. "But I'm not sure your earlobes can handle that sort of strain."

She holds a straight face, but I can see she's on the brink of giggling. "I already stockpiled a pound of Gouda and a set of jumper cables for the Manchurian Twist, but if you'd rather start with the Blinking Lightsaber, I suppose I can look into renting a chainsaw."

I snort and splash my beer on the table. I half expect Lisa

to whip out a dishcloth and start tidying, but she keeps her attention fixed on me. "Nah, let's go straight for the Throbbing Beanstalk," I suggest. "I've already got the inversion table set up in my living room, and the bear grease is just going to go to waste if we don't use it."

She tries and fails to mask a giggle as her eyes flash with mirth. She drums perfectly manicured fingers on the table and pretends to ponder. "Okay, but if you suggest the Crooked Licorice Whip, I'm going to have to pass. It took forever for that last nipple piercing to heal."

I bust out laughing, bested at my own game. God, what is it about this woman? How the hell can she do sophisticated and silly, straight-laced and sexy, all at the same damn time?

I shake my head and study her over the rim of my pint glass. "You know, you're turning out to be a lot different than I thought you'd be."

She grins and takes a sip of her own beer. "I can't say this is what I expected, either, when I dragged you home from the bar."

"Is that a good thing or a bad thing?"

"Good." She sets her glass down, considering. "I needed to break out of my shell. To try new things. I never realized that until I met you."

I nod, wanting to ask more. Wanting to know where she sees herself in a month, a year, five years. If she sees The Test as a temporary game, or a chance to make more life-altering changes.

But I'm spared the embarrassment of asking any of those questions as the waitress arrives with a heaping pile of hot wings and a trough of ranch dressing. "Here's your napkins," she says as she plunks down a pile of scratchy brown paper. "If you need a refill on those beers, we'd better get it now. Karaoke's about to start."

I glance toward the stage to see a skinny guy with a

mullet and a white T-shirt. He's adjusting a microphone and squinting at a screen that will display lyrics for all the songs. I turn back to Lisa. "Which sister does karaoke?"

"Missy. She's the older one. Married to Paul."

"What's her go-to karaoke song?"

She shrugs and picks up a hot wing. "Usually Bette Midler's 'Wind Beneath My Wings.'"

I do my best not to gag, though I'm sure she sees the mirth in my eyes. "Once she did an Adele song after a few tequila shots," Lisa adds. "But yeah, usually it's kind of pretentious-sounding stuff."

"Missy's the taller one, right? And Cassie is the scientist?"

She nods, and I can tell she's surprised I remembered. "Cassie's tried karaoke once," she says. "But that was just because her fiancé was there and she wanted to serenade him."

"What song did she pick?"

Her cheeks pinken, and I know it's not from the spiciness of the wing she just bit into. "She sang, 'When I Think About You I Touch Myself.'"

I laugh and grab a hot wing of my own. It's tangy and spicy and messy, and the thick poblano-spiked sauce coats my fingers. I finish chewing before I ask another question.

"Have you ever thought about what your song would be?"

She shrugs and grabs another wing, clutching it daintily like it's a teacup. There's a smudge of sauce at the corner of her lip, and I ache to brush it away with my thumb. Or my tongue. Or—

"I've had a few song ideas," she says. "Nothing concrete."

I can tell from the way she's avoiding my eyes that she knows exactly what song she'd sing. And that there's a story of some sort behind it. I wait for her to finish licking sauce off her fingertips.

"Wow, these are spicy," she says.

"Too spicy?"

She shakes her head and takes a sip of beer. "Spicier than I'd normally eat, but I like it." She grins and dabs her mouth with a napkin. "Different is good."

I glance at the stage where the mulleted guy is doing a quick sound check. I turn back to Lisa. "So, you've never done karaoke before?"

She shakes her head and reaches for another wing. "Nope."

"Because it's scary?"

"Terrifying." Her gaze locks with mine, and I can tell she knows where I'm going with this.

"But maybe a little exciting, too?" I keep my voice low, ready to back off if she tells me to.

But her eyes flash with intrigue as she takes a cool sip of beer and dabs her mouth with a napkin. "Maybe."

"Okay then," I say. "Time for your next stage of The Test."

# Chapter Eleven

## LISA

My legs are like jelly as I take a deep breath and brace myself.

"Ready?"

I nod in response to the male voice behind me, but I'm not sure I'm ready at all. I'm terrified.

And a little excited, but mostly scared spitless.

"Okay, ladies and gentlemen," the guy says into the mike. "Our next performer is Miss Lisa Michaels singing 'Bootylicious' with a little help from Destiny's Child."

There's a tepid round of applause, and a few leers from the biker guys at the bar. A few feet away, Dax gives me an encouraging smile. Though he offered to do this with me, I had something else in mind.

Something that scares the ever-lovin' hell out of me right now.

"You got this," Dax mouths.

It's not the words but the mouth that sends a bolt of courage through me. Or maybe it's the memory of where that mouth has been, and where I'd like it to be again. The opening notes blast through the speakers on either side of me, a riff on Stevie Nicks's "Edge of Seventeen," and I'm inspired to do my own riff on the opening lines.

"Cassie, can you handle this?" I sing, my voice cracking as I channel my sexually liberated younger sister.

I clear my throat as the beat pulses, and I try not to choke on my own spit. "Missy, can you handle this?"

Okay, so my older sister would be mortified to see me strutting across the stage like a hoochie right now, but isn't that the point? Feeling eyes on me, I attempt a small, sexy wiggle, stumbling when my heel catches on a cord.

My palms are sweating as I watch the lyrics scroll past on a flickering screen. I belt out the next few lines, voice warbling as I try to recall how the tune goes.

*Tender thang*?

*Ready for this jelly*?

What the hell does this song even mean?

My eyes flick to Dax, and I catch his hungry gaze on my ass. I give a little wiggle and remember why I picked this song.

I belt out the next few lines, gaining confidence as Dax's eyes follow me across the stage. I sound more like an injured cat than a sexy R&B singer, but I'm doing this, dammit. I'm up here with the spotlight making my skin sizzle, or maybe that's all Dax. I lock eyes with him as I sing the next words.

"Baby, can you handle this?"

I sway my hips, attempting another booty shake. I'm amazed when I remain upright, and even more amazed when I spin back around to see Dax has moved to the edge of the bench seat. His eyes are feral, hungry, and when I glance at his lap, there's a telltale bulge.

My confidence swells, sending pulse-beats of energy through me.

"My body too bootylicious!" I yelp, no longer worried

that I can't carry a tune. I've got Dax's full attention, and that's all I care about. That, and finishing this song as fast as possible so I can have his hands on me again.

The last notes have barely faded when he's out of his seat and tossing a wad of cash onto the table. He catches my arm amid a smattering of applause, but I barely hear it. My heart thuds in my ears, along with Dax's voice as he steers me toward a dark hallway in the corner of the room.

"Outside," he growls. "Now."

"But—"

"Yes," he says as he pushes through a door and into the cool night air. "You have the most amazing butt I've ever seen, and if I don't get my hands on it in the next ten seconds, I'm going to fucking explode."

We tumble into the alley together, breathless in the crisp night air with the pounding of bass fading as the door clangs shut behind us. We face each other across darkened asphalt, the spicy scent of hot wing sauce clinging to us like pheromones. The heat between us is palpable, and I lick my lips as I look up at Dax. "You liked the song?"

He gives a soft growl and closes the space between us, his body huge and predatory. "That was the hottest fucking thing I've ever seen in my life."

I resist the urge to giggle, knowing it wasn't my singing prowess that got him. It was something else, something almost chemical between us. We're burning up with it, and my flesh feels fiery despite the chill in the air.

"Touch me," I murmur, but I don't need to ask. He's already there.

Dax presses me up against the brick wall of the building, and I glance left to make sure we're alone. The alley dead-ends on the other side of us, but there could be a parade of clowns closing in on us from the street and I wouldn't know.

I probably wouldn't care, either. That's how desperate I

am to feel Dax's hands on me. I would drop my panties on the fifty-yard line at the Super Bowl.

Speaking of panties—

"Give me your hand," I whisper, then grab it anyway. I slide it under my skirt and watch his eyes widen as his fingers graze bare flesh.

"Jesus Christ," he mutters. "You're bare."

I nod as a shiver ripples through me. It's not a chill from my lack of underwear. It's the thrill of knowing I did this with Dax in mind. I left those perfect La Perla skivvies lying on my duvet at home, knowing full well this is how the night would end.

Well, not exactly like this. I guess I didn't see myself getting frisky in an alley, but I have no objections.

"I wasn't brave enough to go braless like you asked," I whisper. "But with a longer skirt, I thought this might be okay."

"Oh, baby." His voice is a growl as his knuckles graze the softness between my legs before sliding around to the back. "This is better than okay. It's fucking fantastic."

I let my head fall against the brick building as Dax kisses his way down my throat and into the V of my shirt. Both hands are under my skirt, and his grip on my ass reminds me of the song.

"Bootylicious," Dax murmurs, reading my thoughts as he kneads my bare ass. "Tell me something."

"Mmm?" It's the closest thing to actual words I can manage. His fingers grip and squeeze and leave my ass cheeks feeling like they're on fire.

"Why'd you pick that song?"

I groan as he nips my earlobe, and my fingers find their way under the hem of his shirt. His back is broad and hard, and it takes me a second to remember he asked a question.

"It's a good song," I manage, gasping as Dax grips my ass

tighter.

"That wasn't the question," he chides. "I wanted to know why you chose it."

"Oh," I gasp as he dips two fingers into the wetness between my legs. I grip his shoulders, dizzy with desire as he swirls the pads of his fingers through my slickness.

"Tell me, Lisa."

"Wha—what? Don't stop."

He swirls the fingers in a gentle circle around my clit, then dips them back into me. I gasp as he draws them out again and heads the other direction this time. His movements are slick and gentle and oh-so-very slow. I part my legs wider, aching for him to keep going. To touch me *there*—

"Is that what you want?" His breath is in my ear, his fingertips scant centimeters from my back door. "You want me to play with your ass?"

The words send shockwaves of desire pulsing through me. I nod because I can't bring myself to say it out loud. To admit that's what I've been dying to try. Where I want him to touch me.

"Dax," I whisper, hoping he won't make me say it out loud. He's *right there*, so close, so poised to give me what I'm craving.

He draws back and looks me in the eye. Our gazes hold like that for a few breathless moments, neither of us saying a word. It's Dax who shatters the silence.

"Later," he says.

I blink. "What?"

"You don't know how badly I want to touch your tight little ass," he growls. "To slide in my finger or my cock and watch you squirm. But your first time?"

I nod, too stunned by his words to answer, or to even be sure it was a question. But he's right, I've never done that before. Booty play? Not for girls like me. But I've wanted to, or at least I do now. I squirm against him, desperate with need.

"Later." He repeats the vow in a thick growl, and I'm not sure whether I'm more excited by what he's promising, or the fact that it's somewhere in the future. That this thing between Dax and me doesn't have an end date just yet.

His breath skims my ear again, and I give a soft little gasp. "But I can still make you scream."

Before I can say a word, he drops to his knees on the asphalt. No padding, no hesitation, just goes for it. Pushing my skirt up around my hips with one hand, he clutches my ass with the other. "I've been dying to taste you," he growls.

Then his mouth is on me. I gasp as swirls of shimmering pleasure pulse through my whole body. "Dax," I gasp, and clutch the back of his head.

His tongue plunges into me, and my knees go weak. He grips my ass tighter, pressing me against his mouth while my spine roots me against the brick wall. I close my eyes, leaning into the sensation as light and color swirl around me. His mouth makes me mindless, teasing, licking, probing.

"Oh God," I gasp, fisting my fingers in his hair. I loosen my grip when he gives a small grunt of pain, but he doesn't stop. His tongue keeps teasing, moving everywhere at once.

Lights flicker behind my eyelids, and a spear of pleasure spikes right through my spine. My whole body stiffens, and I know what's coming.

Me.

"Yes!" My shriek bounces off the brick walls, and I bite my lip to keep from doing it again. But each burst of sensation rocks me back on my heels as Dax strokes and sucks and makes me mindless with his mouth.

I'm still panting as the sensation ebbs and I open my eyes. Dax stands up and yanks out his wallet. I start to spin around, ready to brace my palms against the brick. Ready to feel him slide into me from behind.

But Dax grabs my hip with one hand as he tears open the condom wrapper with his teeth. "No," he says. "I want to see you this time."

I drop my hands to his fly and undo his jeans with alarming speed. I'm dying to feel that thick shaft in my palm again.

"Hurry," I whisper, though he already is. He slides on the condom, then clamps both hands around my hips.

"I want you like this," he growls as he hoists me up and pins me against the wall with his body. I wrap my legs around him, knowing exactly how the choreography goes, even though I've never done this in my life.

He sinks into me in one slick motion, filling me so completely that it's all I can do to keep from crying out. I bite my lip and taste blood, but I don't care. As Dax draws back and drives into me again, my whole body arches to take him in.

"Fuck, you feel good." It's his voice in my ear, but the words echo through my head in my own voice.

*So fucking good.*

That's not even something I'd say, but I'm feeling it now. Experiencing pleasure like I've never felt before.

"Dax." I gasp and grind against him, grateful for the wall at my back, for the delicious angle that lets me grind against him just like that—

"I'm close," I gasp, astonished that it could happen so soon. He drives into me again, and the sensation grips me, yanking me over the edge and into another dizzying bliss spiral.

"God, Lisa," he groans, and I feel him let go, too. His fingers clutch my ass, and he pumps me with such force I see glitter behind my eyelids. He gives a soft groan, and stiffens in my arms, between my legs, driving into me until he's spent.

We both stand there panting for a few heartbeats. Well, he's standing. I'm still pinned against the wall with my legs around his waist, so I slowly lower myself to the ground and tug my skirt down. I straighten my Mötley Crüe shirt and avert my gaze while Dax gets rid of the condom in a nearby dumpster.

The fact that I've just had sex less than five feet from a dumpster should alarm me. It should make me feel like trash.

*Should, should, should—*

How much of my life has been driven by that word?

Dax returns to my side and gives me a smile that's almost sheepish. It's an odd shift from the alpha aggressor who drove into me with such force only seconds ago, and the contrast makes me smile back.

"Hey," I murmur, trying to play it cool.

"Hey back," he says, and kisses the side of my neck. He kisses my chin, too, then presses his lips to mine for the slowest, deepest, softest kiss imaginable. When he draws back, we're both a little starry-eyed.

"Sorry we didn't get to fulfill all your fantasies," he murmurs. "The bootylicious one?"

My cheeks go warm, and I glance down at my toes. "There's still time."

"Definitely. Before this is all over, I promise."

The words are hopeful, but their finality sends me crashing down a wall of disappointment. It shouldn't be that way. We pledged to end this after thirty days. To get what we needed from each other and walk away with a handshake at the end.

Am I starting to change my mind?

I nod, not sure whether I'm answering Dax's question or my own.

"Yes," I whisper. "Before this is all over."

# Chapter Twelve

## Dax

As we climb the steps to the museum, I reach for Lisa's hand. Our fingers lace together like a matched set. It's not until she turns and smiles at me that I realize what a relationshippy thing I've done.

Then again, this *is* sort of a date. Today's outing has nothing to do with The Test, and I'm not sure how to feel about that.

"Here we are," she says, reaching for the front door. "You have the tickets?"

I nod and pat the pocket of my shirt. It's the only dress shirt I own, and I'm not sure what it says that I've donned it today for Lisa. "Got 'em," I tell her. "I still can't believe I let you drag me to some swanky gallery party."

She rolls her eyes and pulls open the door. "I told you, it's not a swanky gallery party. It's an opening for a new art exhibit. One I think you'll really like."

There's a part of me that wants to mutter like a surly

jackass about being cleaned up and towed to a highbrow arts and culture affair like a monkey in a suit.

There's another part of me that loves the idea that Lisa's chosen something special with me in mind. That she put "Dax" and "art" into the same sentence and didn't bust up laughing.

"Come on," she says, pulling me along through the stark white corridor. "The cocktail lines at these things are always huge, so I want to beat the crowd."

"Far be it from me to get between Lisa Michaels and a fancy cocktail."

She grins at me as she turns a corner and halts in front of a large easel. "Here," she says, pointing at the sign. "This is what we're going to see."

I stare at the words, absorbing the significance.

*Wild and Untamed: An Intimate Photographic Exploration of North American Wolves, by Nathaniel Kahn.*

"Wolves," I repeat, too dumbfounded to say anything smarter than that.

"Like your sculpture," she says. "I knew you liked them, so when I saw the ad for this opening, I thought…" She trails off, furrowing her brow as she studies my face. "I'm sorry. Is this not okay?"

I'm not sure what she sees in my expression. Awe? Gratitude? Sadness? All of those things, maybe, but I'm determined not to let it show. "It's awesome," I tell her, which is true. "I'm blown away that you thought of me."

Her smile returns, and she grips my hand again. "I'm so glad. The artist is supposed to be amazing. He's a photographer who works mostly in black and white images, but this is the first time he's done a show of wildlife photography."

"What does he normally do?"

"He specializes in erotic imagery. Very artistic."

"Erotic?"

"Not like that," she says, probably recognizing intrigue in my voice. "It's not porn or anything."

"That's too bad. I kinda like porn."

She rolls her eyes, but I can tell she's not really annoyed. "He usually does abstract, boudoir photography. The sort of thing where you can't tell whether you're looking at a thigh or a shoulder or a breast. Very unique."

"That sounds…confusing."

She grins and pulls me toward the door. "It's mysterious."

We walk into a room filled with well-dressed intellectuals gazing thoughtfully at massive, well-lit photographs. Two men near the door sip from champagne flutes while debating the use of light. Next to them is a woman in a black cocktail dress holding a tiny white dog in a sequined bag. Across from her, a trio of well-dressed hipsters stand with faces tilted upward in that snobby, high-society pose that always sets me on edge.

I'm so busy being a judgmental prick that it takes me a second to notice Lisa has gone strangely pale.

"You okay?"

"Yeah," she murmurs. "I just—I know that guy over there."

I follow the direction of her gaze to a dark-haired man in the corner wearing a crisp navy suit and a bored expression. He looks like old money and probably smells like expensive cologne. I'd rather not get close enough to sniff him. I glance back at Lisa.

"Is that Gary?"

"No." She shakes her head and squeezes my hand. "Stop staring. I don't want him to come over here."

"Who is he?"

"A client," she says, then makes a face. "An *ex*-client. He made a pass at me when his wife was out of town and I was finishing up one of their summer homes. He got kind of aggressive about it."

Everything about that statement irritates me. The fact that this prick tried to screw around on his wife. The fact that he'd try it with Lisa. Hell, I hate that he has multiple summer homes. It's all I can do right now to keep from storming across the room and punching him in his smug-bastard face.

"Come on," Lisa says. "Let's get that drink."

I take a deep breath and pat myself on the back for having the self-control not to hit anyone at a swanky gallery party. I stop patting when I see the guy headed our way.

"Lisa? Lisa Michaels? I thought that was you."

Douchebag struts up to us and leans in like he's going to kiss her cheek. Lisa's grimace is the only cue I need to run interference.

"I'm Dax," I announce, wedging my body between his lips and Lisa's face. I don't bother with a last name. The asshole deserves as few syllables as possible. "I don't think we've met."

I don't extend a handshake, and neither does he. Lisa rests a hand on my back but keeps most of her body tucked behind me. If I had any doubts about whether she's okay with me stepping in, they're erased by that one tiny gesture.

Douchebag stares me down. More like *up*, actually, since I've got a good eight inches on him. "Miles," he says. "Miles Pritchard the Third."

He says it like I'm supposed to be impressed, and I concentrate very hard on channeling the same bored expression he reserved for the artwork. "Miles," I repeat, adding a slight sneer to my voice. "You having a good time here tonight, Miles?"

"Uh—yes, excellent." He tugs at his tie and glances around me at Lisa. "And you?"

"Splendid," Lisa says, nestling up closer. I slide an arm around her, glad she's not pissed at me. Glad she's not having to confront this guy alone.

"Is your lovely wife here with you tonight, Miles?" I ask.

He blanches and shoots a nervous glance at Lisa. "Uh—"

"Gwendolyn," she supplies, like he might have forgotten. "Such a sweetheart," Lisa adds as she gives me a smile I can't quite read. "President of the Women's Charity League. And a wonderful tennis player."

"She sounds terrific," I say. "I think it's important for a man to respect and appreciate his wife, don't you, Miles? Your beautiful, charitable, tennis-playing wife?"

"Um, yes—yes, certainly." Miles appears to very much regret crossing the room. Like if he could hit reverse on his Gucci loafers, he'd back his ass up so fast he'd leave streaks on the carpet.

"Good." I clap him on the shoulder and smile like we're best buddies. "I'm glad we had this talk, aren't you?"

He nods and takes a few steps back, spotting his escape route. "Of course," he says, still backing away. "It was great to see you again, Lisa. And good to meet you—uh—Dex."

"Dax," I tell him, though I'm betting he damn well knows that.

I'm also betting Lisa won't be getting any more business from the guy. I turn to face her as Miles disappears around a corner. "Sorry about that," I mutter. "I hope I didn't screw up a valuable client relationship or anything."

"Are you kidding?" She beams at me, then stands on tiptoe to plant a furtive kiss at the edge of my mouth. She draws back and gives me a shy smile that makes my chest ache. "I was hoping I'd never have to see that guy again."

"I think we made sure of that." I slide my hand over hers and give a small squeeze, glad I didn't make the wrong call. "Let's get you that cocktail."

We step up to the bar, and she orders something that has more ingredients than a bottle of drain cleaner. I get a Jack and Coke, and we move back into the foyer for our first real look at the art on display.

"Wow," Lisa says, tipping her head to stare up at a framed photo that's taller than she is. "That's a big wolf."

I laugh and take a step back to get the full effect. "Nice teeth," I say. "You wouldn't want to meet that guy in a dark alley."

"Mmm," she says, giving me a coy little smile as she lowers her voice to a whisper. "Especially not if you were in that alley without panties."

My dick throbs with the reminder. I can't believe we've reached this point. That we're sharing inside jokes and shared memories as we stand here holding hands in a museum. It's on the tip of my tongue to say something mushy and romantic and utterly unlike me, but Lisa tugs my hand and pulls me toward another photo.

"What do you think of this one?"

The photo shows a shaggy gray wolf staring down a smaller brownish wolf with wideset yellow eyes. It's a stunning image, and it might be two males squaring off to brawl. But I'm pretty sure it's not.

"Is it just me, or is that a smoldering look?" I ask.

"Definitely," she agrees. "I'm guessing that one's the lady wolf?"

"He looks like he wants to jump her bones," I whisper low in Lisa's ear.

She giggles and tilts her head up so her lips brush my ear. "And she looks like she wouldn't mind at all."

I'm about to suggest we skip the rest of the show and go back to my place when a skinny man in a black tie comes rushing toward us with tiny spectacles perched on his nose. "Isn't it spectacular?" he asks.

His expression is friendly enough, and he's so damn earnest I find myself nodding. "Absolutely," I agree, hoping he didn't hear me make that crack about the wolves humping.

"Very…uh, artistic."

"I agree," he says. "It's mesmerizing to see two creatures engaged in the most primal, magnificent display of nature and instinct." He sticks out a hand, which I shake firmly before he grabs Lisa's hand and plants a kiss on her knuckles.

"Sullivan Wainright, editor of *Oregon Art Experience* magazine," he says.

"Lisa Michaels of LM Interior Design," she says. "And this is Dax Kensington."

"Pleasure to meet you." I shoot a glance at Lisa, not sure if I'm supposed to rattle off my business as well, or say something meaningful about the wolves who may or may not be preparing to bump uglies. I settle for gazing thoughtfully at an image of two cinnamon-colored canines curled around each other in a cozy snuggle.

"Don't you just love the raw energy and recognizable emotion in this one?" Sullivan adjusts his glasses. "I love what it says about the circular nature of instinct and survival."

Beside me, Lisa licks her lips and nods. "It's sure something."

"Phenomenal," Sullivan says, swinging his attention back to the first image with the wolves exchanging the heated look. "Such an exquisite display of might and instinct. I love what he's done with the composition here. The statement Kahn is making with his choice in aperture—no other artist could make such a bold critique of societal norms and the way humanity relates to them."

"Uh, yes," Lisa says, biting her lip in a way that tells me she's stifling laughter at the memory of our shared joke. "It's very…um…sensuous."

"Exactly." Sullivan beams like she's gotten an answer right on a test question, and Lisa clears her throat.

"I think I need to visit the ladies' room," she says. "It was wonderful meeting you, Sullivan."

"Likewise," the man says, and steps toward the next image.

Lisa grabs my arm and hurries toward the far side of the room, but stops short to whisper in my ear. I lean down to listen, and to enjoy the tantalizing view down the front of her dress.

"Oh my God," she says, half whispering, half giggling. "We're surrounded by creepers and snobs and wolves making lusty eyes at each other."

Her words make me snort-laugh, and I love that she sounds so delighted. "What a striking artistic observation you've made, Miss Michaels. Would you care to elaborate?"

She smiles up at me, green eyes sparkling with laughter. "Why, yes," she murmurs in a prim little art critic voice. "I'm deeply moved by the saturation and symmetry in that piece next to the fern." She points to an impressively large photo of two Arctic wolves.

It's a damn fine image, and I love that she brought me here to see it. I also love that she's not taking this whole thing too seriously. That she isn't afraid to have fun with it.

"Yes, it's quite exquisite," I agree, adjusting my imaginary monocle as we step in front of an image showing a wolf belly-crawling through the mud. "Don't you find this one here makes a bold statement about focal point and negative space while demonstrating the wolf's underlying need for a good bath and brush?"

She laughs so hard she nearly spills her cocktail. When her gaze meets mine, she bites her lip. "Did I ever tell you I used to volunteer at this museum?"

I shake my head, wondering what that sexy smirk is all about. "You never mentioned it."

"There's an exhibit on the third floor called Oregon Adventure," she says. "It's laid out to look like different cabins so you can get a glimpse of how fur trappers and gold miners and other early Oregon settlers used to live."

"That sounds interesting," I say, not sure how to reconcile this little history lesson with the suggestive gleam in Lisa's eye.

"My first month here, I caught a couple going at it on one of the bunks in the Lewis and Clark exhibit," she says. "They were buck naked, right there between the bearskin rug and the display of nineteenth-century muskets."

Her voice is scandalized, but there's intrigue there, too. Desire. I hold her gaze, pretty sure I get where she's going with this. "Did you say anything to them?"

She nods, cheeks flushed. "Of course. I lectured them for twenty minutes about lewd behavior and the importance of being respectful of culture and public spaces."

I can picture it in my head, and I try not to laugh. "And were they embarrassed?"

"Not at all." There's an awe in her voice that makes me picture it perfectly. Lisa in her heels and pearls, scolding the disheveled couple for their scandalous behavior while deep down, wanting it for herself.

I lean closer, cocktails and wolves and art critics all but forgotten now. "I don't suppose you still have a key to the room?"

She grins, her expression equal parts nervous and excited. "No key necessary. I even know a shortcut."

"Well then," I murmur. "How'd you like to take me on an Oregon Adventure?"

# Chapter Thirteen

## LISA

"What exactly did you used to do here?"

Dax's question makes me giggle, or maybe it's the way his hair tickles the underside of my breast as he kisses his way up my naked torso.

"Definitely not this," I say, then gasp as he shifts his hips to rock deeper inside me. His movements are slow and deliberate, and I'm not sure if he's trying to tease, or trying to avoid jostling the collection of antique frying pans on the wall above the log bed.

"I helped them stage exhibits," I tell him, conscious of the breathiness in my voice. It's not easy carrying on a conversation while having illicit sex in a replica of a cot slept on by members of the Corps of Discovery at Fort Clatsop in 1805. "That, and I gave tours for schoolchildren."

"As a volunteer?"

"Yes," I say, though it comes out more like a hiss. Good Lord, Dax knows how to move. Does he know how freaking good he is at this?

The smug look on his face tells me he does, and also that he plans to torture me for a good long while. He slides in slowly, smiling down into my eyes as he takes his time easing back again.

"And you were also a board member?" he asks like it's the most natural thing in the world to discuss my career history mid-coitus.

I nod and try to recall what he asked me. "Definitely not—bored. What?"

He laughs, and I close my eyes, wanting to contain the sensation of Dax driving deep inside me. Then I open them again, because I really need to see this to get the full effect.

I reach up and tug the tail on his coonskin cap. "I promise this isn't a priceless artifact. I bought it at a thrift store in the Pearl District when I helped stage this exhibit."

"You're so fucking smart," he murmurs. "Why is that such a turn-on?"

"Beats me. But I'm glad it is."

Dax shifts again, taking his time sliding in and out of me. It's a delicious tease, though probably ill-advised since there are a hundred art connoisseurs milling around two floors below us. The only reason I'm not freaking out is that I know this floor is closed to the public tonight.

"Oh," I gasp as he flicks his tongue over my nipple again. "That's nice."

"Careful," he warns as I grip the log bedpost. "If you knock that bearskin rug off the wall, I'll have nightmares for years about being attacked by a grizzly."

"It's a black bear," I murmur and grip his shoulder instead of the bedpost. "One of a hundred and twenty-two animals catalogued during the Lewis and Clark Expedition between eighteen-*oh*-four and eighteen-oh-sex."

"Sex?" He grins down at me as he moves his hips to hit

something really deep inside me. I arch up, forgetting about bears and muskets and history and pretty much everything else but the way Dax feels inside me.

But he's there to remind me. "Tell me more about Lewis and Clark."

I open my eyes and study him. "Is this your idea of dirty talk?"

"Kind of." He grins down at me as he slides out and back in again, deliciously hard and slick. "Let's just say I'm developing a fetish for hot brainy babes."

"Plural?" I give him a teasing, haughty look, but he breaks my concentration as he moves again. His mouth dips into the hollow between my ear and shoulder, and the warmth of his breath sends an army of goose bumps marching down my arm.

Or maybe that's the wall of mounted animal heads on the wall across from us. I glance away and focus on answering Dax's question. "The leaders of the expedition were Captain Meriwether Lewis and Second Lieutenant William Clark," I tell him.

"Meriwether? I'll bet his wife had a helluva time screaming that in bed."

I giggle and arch up against him, a moan escaping my lips. "He wasn't married, but Toussaint Charbonneau was. He was one of their interpreters, and his wife was Sacagawea."

"Ah, Sacagawea. I've heard of her."

"She taught the explorers about which berries and roots they could eat so they didn't all die of scurvy."

"Scurvy," Dax murmurs, kissing my throat as he eases deeper, distracting me once more with delicious sensation. "Pretty sure that's the first time anyone's said *scurvy* to me during sex."

"How about blunderbuss?"

That stops him short, which is a pity. I liked the way he

was moving. Reading my mind, he starts again, driving up with aching deliberateness. "Blunderbuss?"

I stifle a giggle and a moan at the same time, which is damn hard to do. "It's a kind of rifle the explorers carried. Named for the Dutch words 'thunder gun.' It had a heavy stock, short barrel, and wide-mouthed muzzle."

"Mmm," Dax says, brushing a kiss across my lips as he presses deeper into me. "Speaking of mouths, yours is delicious."

My giggle turns into a moan as he tilts his pelvis just a little, hitting something really good. Pulses of pleasure race through my core, and I know I'm getting closer. There's a delicious buzz building slowly in the center of my body, and I struggle to form coherent thoughts. "Did you know Lewis and Clark had a sextant on their journey?"

"Is that like a threesome, or a special teepee for fucking?"

"Neither," I gasp, recognizing the first tingle of orgasm building inside me. The rest of my explanation comes out in a tangled rush. "It's a special instrument used to make astronomical observations to help calculate distances."

All the words run together, and I'm pretty sure he has no idea what I just said. For that matter, neither do I. All I care about right now is that Dax keeps moving like that, hips thrusting, body creating dizzying friction at the place where we're joined. I arch up against him, so close I can hear my pulse fluttering in my ears.

"Want to hear a Lewis and Clark joke?" he murmurs, his voice low and rumbly in my ear.

"Wha—what?" I think he said something about a joke, but for all I know he asked me to rub off my eyebrows with sandpaper. I'll agree, as long as he keeps doing what he's doing.

"A Lewis and Clark joke," he repeats, his breath warm against my throat. "I learned it in grade school."

"Yes!" I gasp and tighten my legs around Dax, wondering if he knows I'm right on the brink. That if he moves even a little, he'll tip me right over the edge.

"What did Lewis and Clark say when they finally reached the Pacific Ocean?" he asks.

I'm so far gone I can't form words, but I choke out something that sounds like "what?"

Or maybe "don't stop fucking me," I'm not sure. I bite my arm to keep from crying out as the first wave hits me.

"Long time, no sea."

I burst out laughing, right as the orgasm grabs hold. The result is a dizzying combination of gasping and giggling and thrusting and breathless, giddy hysterics.

*Holy mother of hell, who knew a laughing orgasm was a thing?*

By the time I come down, I'm practically hyperventilating. Tears are running down my face and Dax reaches down to wipe one from my lashes. He grins down at me, a little breathless from his own release. "I knew that would come in handy someday."

"Oh God," I gasp, still struggling to catch my breath. "I don't know if I've ever laughed so hard in bed."

"Most guys would take offense to that."

But he isn't most guys. In every way possible, in all the best ways, Dax Kensington is *not* most guys.

And somewhere deep down, I know that will make it harder to say goodbye when The Test is done.

• • •

Later that week, my sisters come over for wine, gossip, and friendship salad.

"Please stop calling it that," Cassie groans as she plunks down a limp-looking carrot, a head of broccoli, and something that looks suspiciously like a baggie of Cheetos. "Friendship salad makes it sound like we're going to hold hands and sing 'Kumbaya' over a plate of arugula."

"Well, we might if someone had thought to bring arugula," Missy huffs as she eyes Cassie's offerings with disdain before arranging herself on one of my leather barstools at the edge of my granite island. "Luckily, I brought kohlrabi, shredded beets, green onion, and a half-pound of Brussel sprouts that I slow-roasted with pancetta and Medjool dates to lend a sweet-smoky flavor."

"Lucky us," Cassie mutters, though she's smiling as she reaches over and steals a piece of pancetta out of Missy's Tupperware container. Missy smacks her hand, and Cassie yelps with indignation.

"Sorry I'm late!" Sarah Keating bursts through the front door, her long caramel hair flying behind her and a phallic object in her hand. "Does anyone else feel self-conscious shopping for cucumbers? Like you're standing there squeezing them and checking out the length and girth to make sure you get the best one, and you look over to see every creepy guy in the produce section is staring at you."

Cassie snort-laughs, while Missy tries—and fails—to look appalled. "That has never in a million years crossed my mind," Missy says. "But that's a very nice-looking cucumber. English, right?"

"Beats me." Sarah arranges herself on the barstool next to Cassie, while Missy reaches over to pour her a glass of Pinot Noir.

"Where's Junie?" Cassie asks.

Sarah is a case manager at the group home where Junie lives, which is how we all know her. In the year-and-a-half since Cassie and Simon met, we've become quite tight.

"Simon called and said they got stuck in traffic coming back from the Mariners game." Sarah takes a sip of wine.

"He'll bring her straight here."

"Poll time," Cassie says, reaching out to pluck one of my smoked salmon canapes off the platter in front of Sarah. "Is the name 'friendship salad' the stupidest thing you've ever heard, or the second stupidest thing you've ever heard?"

Missy frowns. "What would the first be?"

Sarah rolls her eyes and grabs a canape of her own. "'I think we're better off as good friends, don't you?'" she quips.

"Ouch." Cassie grimaces and gives me a look I recognize as my cue to open another bottle of wine.

I hesitate, wanting to hear the rest of the story. "I take it that's the big talk Keith wanted to have last night?"

Sarah nods and says around a mouthful of canape, "Yep."

"Oh, honey." Missy reaches out and pats her hand. "I know you were hoping he was going to ask you to move in."

Sarah shrugs and wipes her mouth with the back of her hand before I can pass her one of my hand-embroidered linen napkins. "Another one bites the dust." She picks up her wineglass and takes a fortifying sip. "You guys are sick of hearing about my stupid breakups, and I don't feel like talking about it anyway." She pastes on a shaky smile and turns to Cassie. "What were you saying about friendship salad?"

When Cassie hesitates, Sarah gives her a good-natured nudge with her elbow. "I'm serious, I'm fine," she says. "I don't want to be that girl who's always talking about her lousy breakups at girls' night. So, friendship salad?"

I grab the conversational baton and run with it. "Cassie thinks it's a dumb name, but I happen to like the idea."

"I like the *idea*," Cassie says. "Just not the name."

"Spoken by the woman whose contributions look like something pillaged from the crisper drawer in a frat house," Missy retorts.

Cassie shrugs and bites into a crudité. "What can I say? I've been in Baker City all week testing soil pH levels at a former landfill site, and then I spent two days catching up with Simon."

"I'm not sure we need to know what 'catching up' is code for," Sarah says with a grin. "That's my boss we're talking about."

Cassie flushes with pleasure while I set to work chopping the artichoke hearts I've marinated all week in a special blend of lemon, bay leaves, olive oil, and juniper berries. "Anyway, I happen to love friendship salad," I say. "I adore the idea of all of us contributing something to make a great big salad filled with a little love from everyone."

Cassie pretends to gag, but I know she doesn't mean it. Her pores practically ooze love. I've seen the way she and Simon make goo-goo eyes at each other when no one's looking. There's lust, sure, but also a mix of respect and love and affection that takes my breath away sometimes.

"I want that," I say out loud.

The three women look at me, then each other.

"The limp carrot?" Missy points and starts to hand it to me, but I shake my head.

"No, I'll pass on that. I meant— Never mind."

Hell. I didn't mean to bring this up. To talk about my growing feelings for Dax. But the way my sisters are eyeing me says they'll get it out of me one way or another.

"Speaking of limp carrots, how are things with Dax?" Sarah says with a faux casual air.

I give an unladylike snort-laugh and grab a radish off the sideboard. "His carrot is most definitely *not* limp," I assure her. "And honestly, it's more like a late-season zephyr squash or a Costata Romanesco zucchini."

Missy's eyes widen, while Cassie busts out laughing and swipes a slice of radish off my cutting board. "I thought you had that look about you."

"What do you mean?" I demand, swatting her away from

my pile of thinly sliced veggies.

"You're all cheerful and glowing lately," Cassie says. "Like a woman getting laid well and often."

Sarah grins and heaves an intentionally dramatic sigh. "Lucky bitch."

It's the nicest compliment anyone's paid me in a long time, and I try not to let it show how pleased I am.

Ever the peacemaker, Missy reaches across the counter to pat Sarah's hand. "Someday your prince will come."

"And then, so will you," Cassie adds. "Over and over and over—"

"Why didn't you ever tell me about the multiple orgasm thing?" I blurt out the question before thinking it through, but I don't regret it. Honestly, I like that I finally have something substantial to bring to the table of girl talk.

Three pairs of eyes swing to me, and everyone stops laughing. "What?" Missy says.

Heat creeps into my cheeks, but I'm determined to press on with the risqué girl talk. I've never been part of it this way. I've listened, sure, but I haven't had something noteworthy to contribute until now.

"I—uh—I guess I never realized it was possible to—" I give a flourished gesture with the knife, hoping at least one of them will fill in the blank.

Cassie grins and picks up her wineglass. "I'm pretty sure I've mentioned—" She gives an exaggerated flourish to mimic mine, making my cheeks heat up again. "So to speak," she adds. "Didn't you believe me?"

I shake my head, torn between feeling embarrassed and excited. Like I'm part of the club or something. "I guess I never realized," I say. "I never thought it could be like that."

Missy studies my face, her eagle eyes missing nothing. "You're talking about sex, right? Just sex? That's still all it is?"

They're all watching me, like they know the secret thoughts I've been having all week. Like when Dax called Tuesday night to make sure I got home safely from a job over in Gresham, and we stayed on the phone talking until almost midnight. It wasn't even phone sex, which—FYI—should probably be on my sexual bucket list.

If I keep adding things, maybe The Test will never end? Like maybe I could propose an extension beyond the thirty days we agreed to at the start.

The ladies are still staring, so I force myself to keep a neutral expression as I pick up Cassie's carrot and start to peel it.

"Right," I say slowly. "It's still just sex."

I focus all my attention on the carrot, reminding myself to keep it that way. Sex without love, that's what we agreed.

There's a knock at the door, and Sarah glances down at her phone. "Oh, that's Simon and Junie."

"Don't worry, I already told him he can't stay," Cassie says. "This is girls' night. He's just dropping off Junie."

But as she gets up and opens the door for him, it's clear she's thrilled to bits to lay eyes on her fiancé. Her whole body seems to float, and she greets him like they've been apart six years instead of six hours.

Lucky bitch, indeed.

"Hi, everybody!" Junie says as she hustles into the room. Her T-shirt is emblazoned with an electric guitar, the logo for the National Down Syndrome Association, and the words, *"I'm rockin' this extra chromosome."* She marches in wearing a Mariners cap and holding a plastic bag of produce. "I told Simon to stop at the store so I could buy things for the friendship salad," she announces as she thrusts the bag at me.

"That's perfect, Junie, thank you." As I stretch my hand out for the bag of tomatoes, she studies my face with interest.

"You're in love?" Junie's expression is earnest, and her

words so startling they halt the rest of the conversation in the room. Everyone stops talking at once. The room goes silent, and all eyes fix on me again.

"What?" My cheeks go hot, and I suspect they're the same color as these tomatoes. "No, of course not. Why do you think that?" I glance from Missy to Cassie to Simon and back to Junie again, waiting for one of them to rescue me.

Unfazed, Junie continues to study me with intense curiosity. "I think you love somebody," she says. "You look like you do. Like when Simon and Cassie started to love each other that way."

My cheeks go hotter, and I decide to focus on the tomatoes. I set to work washing them—the tomatoes, not my cheeks—and hope no one notices how awkward I'm being. "I've been dating a man, sure, but it's nothing serious," I say in a breezy tone that sounds like I sucked on a helium balloon. "You met Dax. The guy with the motorcycle? He's really just a good friend."

My voice wobbles a little, and I'm certain it doesn't go unnoticed. I glance up to see Junie smiling like she's just uncovered life's greatest truth. "You love him," she repeats.

It's a statement this time, not a question, and there's a part of me that can't help but wonder if she's onto something.

"Come on," I say, desperate to change the subject. "Let's get this salad put together so we can eat."

Junie smiles, and my stomach does a funny somersault.

I'm pretty sure I'm fooling no one, least of all myself.

# Chapter Fourteen

## Dax

The phone rings at noon on Wednesday, and I'm annoyed with myself for feeling so damn elated to see Lisa's name.

"Hello, hot stuff," I say.

She laughs, and I flip up the shield up on my welding visor and wonder what she's wearing.

"Hello—crap, I can't think of any good pet names for you," she answers.

"Pookie?" I offer.

"Ew."

"Custard bunny?"

"Gross."

"My steaming hunk of man meat?"

She laughs again, and it's a sound that leaves my body humming. I settle back against the workbench in my warehouse and set down the welding torch I was messing with when she called.

"Now I've forgotten why I called you," she says.

"It wasn't just to hear my sexy voice?" I say. "Or for phone sex?"

"That's a terrific idea, actually," she says. "Can we schedule that in sometime before The Test is over?"

"You don't schedule phone sex, Lisa." I ignore the pang in my gut that comes from thinking of The Test ending. I'm not ready for that yet, and we still have ten days to go. "It's not something you put in your day planner and color code with stickers."

She giggles again, and I think I could do this forever. Not just cracking jokes on the phone to make her laugh, but *this*. This easy camaraderie and companionship filled with humor and banter and lots and lots of good sex.

"So, what's up?" I ask, figuring I should get on with it before I go too far down that rabbit hole.

"Well, next week is my birthday."

"Oh. Shit, I should have known that, huh?"

"No, no—that's not what I meant. I'm not fishing for gifts or anything. I usually keep my birthday low-key. Maybe a spa getaway with my sisters or an overnight trip to some luxury resort."

"That's your idea of low-key?"

She sighs, but I can tell she's not really pissed. How have I reached this point where I can read her demeanor over the phone without a single word?

"In honor of The Test, I had an idea for something I'd like to try for my birthday," she says. "I was hoping you could help with that."

"Sure," I say, sitting up a little straighter. "Whatever you want. Anything."

*Jesus, Kensington. Desperate much?*

I clear my throat and try to play it cool. "What did you have in mind?"

"Well, I've been thinking about roughing it."

"Roughing it?" Visions of whips and chains swirl through my head, and I imagine Lisa tied spread-eagle on my bed with silk scarves.

"Not like that," Lisa says, and I wonder if she's read my thoughts. "Camping," she says. "I've never gone camping, and I thought I'd like to try it."

"Camping," I repeat, erasing the spreader bars from my brain and replacing them with tent poles. "You've never been camping?"

"Not once. And you seem like the kind of guy who'd know how."

"There's not much to it, really," I say. "Just throw a tent and some sleeping bags in the car, pack a cooler with camping food, and head out into the wilderness."

"That sounds so—exotic."

I smile to myself, charmed by how easy it is to impress her. To introduce her to something totally mundane and have her experience it for the first time. Forget the antiquated triumph of deflowering some simpering virgin. The thrill of de-virginizing Lisa with an array of new life experiences beats that hands down.

"So how about next weekend?" I suggest, restraining myself from suggesting we jump in the car right this second and drive off into the mountains together. "Are you free?"

"That's what I was hoping you'd say. My birthday is Saturday, and I like the idea of falling asleep under the stars."

I picture myself there beside her, the two of us snuggled up inside sleeping bags zipped together. Her bare ass is cradled spoon-style against me, and her hair smells like campfire.

I tell myself to knock it off when I catch myself inhaling.

"That sounds perfect," I say. "I have all the gear—tent, sleeping bags, air mattress, camp stove—the whole works. I'll even get the sleeping bags dry cleaned before we head out."

"Oh," she says, like the thought hadn't occurred to her.

"You have a pair of sleeping bags. Does one of them belong to Kaitlyn or something?"

I bark out a laugh, not sure if I'm more surprised she remembers my ex's name or at the idea of Kaitlyn going camping.

"Kaitlyn has definitely never been camping," I tell her. "You're one up on her there."

And in so many other ways, I think but don't say.

"Well. Okay, that's good. I mean—I'm glad." She sounds flustered, and I think about how strange this must be for her. In a quest for new experiences, is she ever worried about losing herself?

"I can bring the camping food," she offers. "I have a cooler I've taken to potlucks, and there's this great cookbook I found on haute cuisine for campfires."

"Is that a fancy way of saying hot dogs?"

"No hot dogs," she says. "But I definitely have a surprise or two planned."

My heart speeds up, and I wonder what she has in mind. Is it sexy, culinary, or something else entirely?

Truthfully, I don't care. I'm just excited to spend a whole weekend with her.

*Keep it together*, I remind myself. *Don't get carried away.*

Deep down, I think it might be too late for that.

I think I'm falling for Lisa Michaels.

# Chapter Fifteen

LISA

"Aren't you glad I made you go back and change clothes?"

Dax's words are teasing, not smug, but I still seize the opportunity to smack his shoulder before I return to the task of scraping melted marshmallow off the sleeve of my sweatshirt.

"Fine," I say, ignoring the desire that flutters through me from contact with his shoulder. Good Lord, the man is ripped. "You're right that it's a lot easier to get marshmallow out of fleece than cashmere."

"And aren't those sneakers more comfortable than those high heels would have been?"

"They weren't high heels, they were wedges. But yes," I admit grudgingly. "I'm glad you had me change clothes."

"And I'm glad you let me watch."

"Even if it did result in us hitting the road an hour late."

"Totally worth it." Dax grins, then bends down to add another log to the campfire. He stirs things around with a stick, giving me another chance to appreciate those deliciously broad shoulders, which are visible even through his lumberjack flannel.

He sits back, and I try to pretend I wasn't staring. I focus instead on arranging the perfect layers of chocolate on my graham cracker, while he reaches into the Tupperware container for another marshmallow. "I still can't believe you made marshmallows from scratch."

"And graham crackers," I point out. "And the Guittard Ambanja chocolate is way better than that Hershey's crap you wanted to bring."

"Bonus points on the food," he says. "Does that make us even?"

"Maybe. You haven't tried the wine yet."

He laughs and reaches for the decanter. "For future reference, most people bring cans of beer and Dinty Moore stew when they camp," he says. "Not an entire Riedel stemware set and an eighty-dollar bottle of port."

"Taste it."

Dax pours us each a glass and takes a sip. "Damn," he says, eyes wide. "What is that?"

"It's a 2007 Ferreira vintage port dessert wine from Portugal." I beam, pleased to have nailed it, even if I did overdo things just a little. "I polled my wine club on the best possible wine pairing to go with s'mores, and that was the winner."

He shakes his head and threads another marshmallow onto his roasting stick. "That is fucking amazing," he says. "So are you, by the way. You've made the best camping meal I've ever had in my life. Maybe the best meal I've had, period."

"Thank you." I try not to beam too wide. I know it should rankle my inner feminist to have a man praise my culinary prowess, but you know what? I'm a damn fine chef, and a kickass domestic goddess all around. It feels good to be acknowledged for it.

It also feels good to have Dax slide his arm around my shoulder as he extends his roasting stick into the fire. We're quiet, which is pleasant, too. Crickets chirp in the distance, and the smell of wood smoke and pine needles swirls around us in a fragrant cloud. Darkness is falling, bringing with it vast swaths of stars strung across the sky like twinkle lights. It's as though we're the only two people on the planet. I shift in my camp chair—another thing I had no idea existed—and lean into the warmth of Dax's body.

"Do you want to know about the wolf?"

His voice is so low that I almost don't understand the question at first. I glance up to see him staring into the fire. His jaw is set, and I'm not quite sure how to read him.

"The one in your studio, you mean?" I ask. "Your sculpture?"

"Right. But I meant the story behind it."

"Oh. You said it was your high school mascot?"

"Yes, but that's not the whole story."

He takes a deep breath, and I wait. Something tells me the words he's about to say don't come easily. That there's a reason he wants to share this story. The hairs on my arm prickle, and I know I can't blame the chill blowing off the lake.

"My mom ran off when I was ten, so it was just my brother, my sister, my dad, and me living by ourselves in this tiny little trailer at the scrapyard."

I rest a hand on his knee. "That must have been hard."

Losing his mother, I mean, but all of it. The trailer, the scrapyard, the sort of poverty he's alluded to. I don't get the sense Dax had the best childhood.

He nods and continues. "We'd had a rash of thefts at the junkyard. Sounds stupid, but it's actually pretty common—

junkies stealing scrap metal to sell it. Anyway, my old man decided we needed a guard dog, so he went out and got the meanest sounding dog he could find. Some sort of cross between a pit bull and a wolf."

"Is that even legal?"

"Probably not, but that never stopped my old man." Dax clears his throat. "Anyway, the dog looked all wolf to me. Killer was his name."

"Killer?"

"Yeah. Unfortunately, he didn't live up to that name."

"How do you mean?"

A log rolls over in the fire, and he takes his time rearranging it. My s'more sits forgotten on a napkin in my lap, and I find myself holding my breath as I wait for the rest of the story.

"Killer turned out to be a total teddy bear," Dax says. "Loved belly rubs and dog biscuits and wrestling with kids. Sweetest dog you ever met in your life."

The softness of his voice washes over me in waves as flames flicker in my peripheral vision. I can picture it in my mind—a huge, furry body with a wagging tail and a goofy, wolfy smile. I imagine ten-year-old Dax with his arms around the shaggy neck, a smile on his face for the first time since his mother left.

"What happened to Killer?"

The second the words leave my mouth, I know without being told that this story doesn't have a happy ending.

He doesn't answer right away. "My dad said he was getting rid of him," he says. "Said he wasn't keeping some pussy puppy dog around."

"Oh God."

Tears prick the backs of my eyes as Dax keeps talking. "Took his hunting rifle and the dog and drove off in his shitty pickup truck. When he came back, he had a fifth of whiskey and no Killer. I didn't ask questions."

"Oh, Dax." Tears spill down my cheeks, and I reach over to grab his hand. I clutch it so tight I worry I'm hurting him, but he doesn't seem to notice. He also doesn't notice his marshmallow is starting to smolder. I say nothing, letting it burn. I'll make him a whole tray of marshmallows. Pounds of them, as many as he can eat.

"I'm so sorry," I tell him. "I don't know what else to say."

He shrugs and turns back to me. Noticing the tears, he reaches up and wipes them away with his thumb. His ice-blue eyes flicker with the reflection of the flames. "I've never told anyone that story."

I swallow hard, wishing I had some comforting words to offer. Something that could make it all better. "Thank you for sharing it with me."

He nods. "I wanted you to know. About how I grew up. About why I am the way I am. Why I don't believe in happily-ever-afters."

His words are dark, and there's a thick knot in my throat. I swallow hard to get it to move. "Is that why you volunteer at Helping Paws?"

He nods once, though there's a tiny flicker of surprise in his eyes. "Yeah, I guess so. I can't bring myself to get a dog of my own—not after that. But I feel like I want to give back, you know?"

"I love that about you." I squeeze his hand. "So much."

His eyes flash again, and it's not the fire this time. I replay my words in my head. Did he think I said I love you?

Is that what I meant?

"Your marshmallow." I stand up and pry the roasting stick from his hand. "It's looking a little charred. Here, let me get you another one."

I fumble with the stick, shaking the burned marshmallow into the flames and replacing it with a fresh one.

"Ow." I suck in a breath as melted marshmallow goo sticks to my hand, and I reach for a wet wipe to get it off.

But Dax grabs my wrist and draws my hand to his mouth. "Here, let me." Slowly, so gently, he draws my fingers into his mouth. It's the strangest mix of sexy and soothing, and I catch myself giving a little sigh as the burn ebbs away.

"Better?"

I nod, mesmerized by the flames and by his closeness. "Much better."

He looks at me again, heat in his eyes that has nothing to do with the fire. "Let's try the other hand."

He grabs my left wrist this time, drawing my index and middle finger into his mouth with aching slowness. His tongue grazes the junction of the two fingers, and I gasp from the implication.

Drawing back, he smiles. I don't know why, but I feel like something's shifted between us. A connection on some level we've never visited before.

The heat in his eyes tells me he's aching for a different kind of connection. The one we've almost perfected over the last three weeks.

I shiver, wanting it, too. Wanting it so badly my body aches from it.

"Come on," Dax says. "Let's put this fire out and then check the view from the tent."

# Chapter Sixteen

## DAX

Lisa arches her spine and tilts her face toward the sky, breasts bathed in moonlight as she moves on top of me. I grip her hips, enjoying the show almost as much as I enjoy being buried deep inside her right now.

"Dax," she gasps, and I know I could never get tired of her saying my name.

Especially when she says it like *that*.

She's doing this unreal circular thing with her hips while her back arches so I can slide in deeper.

"That's it," I urge, watching her face for cues she's close. Her gaze is lifted upward, eyes fixed on the night sky. I left the rain fly off on purpose, taking my chances that a downpour is unlikely here in Oregon's high desert. I wanted to see the stars, but watching Lisa enjoy them is even better.

"Oh," she gasps as I arch my pelvis to drive deeper into her. In three weeks, I've learned every nuance of her body. I've learned how her breathing grows ragged right before she comes. I've learned her left breast is a tiny bit bigger than the right. I've learned that if I drive up at just the right time, I can hit her G-spot.

"God, you're beautiful."

She drags her gaze off the stars and looks down at me with a smile. "Thank you. *Oh!*"

There. That blend of perfect manners and unbridled passion. That's what I love about her.

Love?

No. I shake the word out of my head and focus on making her feel good. Making me feel good, too. The sight of her bare breasts dappled in moonbeams, with her blond hair bright against the night sky is going to make me come faster than the way she's riding me now, hips moving faster as she nears the crest.

"Just like that," I whisper. "That's it, baby."

"I'm close."

"I'm right there with you."

And I am, but not just that way. I want to stay inside her like this forever, or at least pretend forever is an option. That it's a word in my vocabulary.

I rock into her again, and that's all it takes.

"Don't stop!"

That's it. The throaty little moan she makes when she's close. I drive up harder, gripping her hips to make sure I hit exactly the right spot.

She goes off like a firecracker, sparks flashing in her eyes as she cries out and throws her head back, riding me hard and fast and slick as I drive into her and come my brains out, too.

She collapses, breathless, on top of me, and I swear to God I could stay like this forever.

But I'm worried about her legs falling asleep, so I ease her to the side and then pull her body to me so she's snug against my chest. She rolls onto one hip and we lie there panting in the darkness, both of us watching the night sky through the top of the tent.

"There!" Lisa points at the sky, eyes wide. "I saw a shooting star."

"Yeah?" I smile and snuggle her closer, loving how soft she feels. "Did you make a wish?"

"Maybe." She looks at me through her lashes with a smile that's almost shy, and I'd give anything to know what she wished for. What she's thinking.

We fall silent again, but there's a whirl of words in my head. What if we really could make this work? What if we didn't say goodbye at the end of this?

"Lisa?"

"Yes?"

I've started the conversation before I've thought of what to say and how to say it. There's a moment where my brain tries to come up with some other topic. Some way to hide what I really want to ask.

"What do you want in the future?"

God, that sounded stupid. Like a college admissions interview—not that I ever did one. I can tell from her expression that she has no idea what I just asked her, and come to think of it, neither do I.

"Well," she says slowly. "I guess I'd like to continue building my business. Developing my skills and becoming the best interior designer I can possibly be."

I nod, appreciating the safe answer. I could stop this conversation right now. Forget I ever tried to broach this sticky subject.

But something urges me to keep going. "What about the rest? Now that you've spent all this time testing your instincts, your life choices, things like that. Is anything—different?"

I need to just shut up. I don't think either of us has the faintest idea what I'm driving at.

*You do. You're just too chickenshit to spit it out.*

Lisa's expression is guarded, and I wonder if she thinks this is a trick question. "I suppose so," she murmurs. "A lot of the things I always thought I wanted aren't the things I actually need."

"Like what?"

"Perfection," she says. "The designer wardrobe. Luxury everything. Being seen at all the best events by all the best people." She makes air quotes around *best events* and *best people*, and I appreciate the self-deprecation in her tone. Her expression softens, then, as she strokes a hand down my chest. "Some of that's necessary for my career, I guess. But what I've realized is that those things don't make me happy. Not really."

"What does make you happy?"

I hold my breath, waiting for her answer. Not sure I can handle it no matter what she says. She's quiet for such a long time that I wonder if she's going to answer at all. When she tips her head back to look up at me, the softness of her smile makes my heart clench like a fist.

"This," she says. "I'm happy right now. Happier than I've ever been."

"Just in this moment, or—?"

I trail off, not sure what I'm asking. If I'm trying to propose something beyond a short fling, or just to get a feel for whether her priorities have changed. If she's wondering, like I am, if we could be this happy for a longer term.

*Grow some balls and say what you want. Tell her, goddammit. Tell her you want more than a fling.*

The instant her expression changes, I know something's wrong. Did she read my mind, or was it something I said? I open my mouth to apologize when her brow furrows in confusion.

"Do you hear that?" she asks.

"Hear what?"

"That hissing sound?" She's silent a moment. "There!"

I listen. Sure enough, she's right. There's something hissing in the back corner of the tent. I sit up and frown, trying to remember if we left the tent open at any point today. There was that one span of time when we were zipping the sleeping bags together, and then when we had to run back to the car for pillows—

"Move over there," I command, pointing to the opposite corner. The one closest to the door and farthest from the corner. "Please," I add, not wanting to be a bossy asshole, but needing her to get her beautiful, naked butt away from that hiss as quickly as possible.

"Why?" Her voice is shaky, but she does it.

I grab my heavy utility flashlight from beside my pillow and edge closer to the corner. "There are a lot of rattlesnakes in this part of the state. I want to be sure we didn't—"

"*Snakes?!*" The word comes out in a bloodcurdling screech, and Lisa is on her feet in an instant. "OhmygodIhatesnakes."

She's flailing and jumping and fumbling for the zipper at the tent door. It would be funny if I weren't afraid for her safety and mine. She's got it unzipped now, but her feet are tangled up in the sleeping bag, which saves her from running naked into the darkness.

It's then I realize the hissing is getting faster.

I grab her by the arm and yank her back down. "Stop screaming," I say. "There—is it louder?"

She's wild-eyed and panting and ready to run like hell the second I let go of her. "Yes—ohmygod, does that mean it's close?"

I edge past her and move toward the corner, pretty sure I know what's up. I pull back the edge of the sleeping bag and aim the beam of my flashlight at the corner.

"There," I say, relieved to be right.

"What? A snake?"

I stretch my hand out to touch it, and Lisa flinches beside me.

"Congratulations," I tell her. "We killed it."

"What? Killed what, the snake?"

"Nope." I turn and grin at her. "The air mattress. Time of death—" I glance at my watch. "Ten forty-three p.m."

"Oh shit."

She stretches out to look, watching as the tag from the sleeping bag flutters in the air that's escaping the mattress at an alarming rate. I grin and pull her against me, toppling us both back onto our rapidly deflating air mattress. Honestly, I don't care. I could sleep naked in the dirt and be happy as long as Lisa's with me.

She giggles and snuggles against me as we descend into the sinking surface. "It's fine," I tell her. "I think I even have a patch kit in the truck."

"I can't believe that."

"What? That we almost died from a nonexistent snake, or that we fucked our air mattress to death?"

"No, you," she says, propping her chin on my chest. "You were going to face down a vicious rattlesnake to save me."

I laugh, appreciating what a noble view of me she has. "Anything for you, babe."

She smiles and folds herself into my arms, sighing as the air continues to billow from our mattress. My butt sinks to the ground, and I'm going to have a killer backache tomorrow, but right now, I don't care.

Right now, in this moment with Lisa, is the happiest I've ever been in my life.

# Chapter Seventeen

LISA

Something changes after the camping trip, though I'm not sure how to describe it exactly.

Some of it is easy to pinpoint—the way Dax sleeps over instead of rushing home, or the way he invites me to join the crew when Helping Paws gets an unexpected influx of bedraggled dogs from a puppy mill in Corvallis.

Some of it is harder to describe. It's a feeling, I guess. The way he steals glimpses at me when we're driving somewhere together, or the way he holds my hand under the table when we have dinner with Cassie and Simon.

"I really like your boyfriend," Cassie whispered when we were leaving, though the extra glass of port she enjoyed over dessert made it more of a loud hiss than a whisper. I know Dax heard her, but neither of us bothered to correct her.

Is that what he was trying to say in the tent? That he wanted to have an actual relationship? I'm not sure, and I'm almost afraid to ask. Afraid that's what I want, and that I won't actually get it if I voice the desire out loud.

Besides, I spent my entire twenties desperate to get married. Isn't part of The Test supposed to be me learning how *not* to be in a relationship?

That doesn't stop me from wanting it, specifically with Dax.

"Whatcha thinking?"

I shake off my daydream and see him regarding me with curiosity from across the table. We're eating corndogs in the AfriCafe at the Oregon Zoo, sandwiched between the Elephant Plaza and the Predators of the Serengeti exhibit.

"I'm thinking the zoo was a really great idea."

He laughs and swirls his corndog through a puddle of ketchup. "Way to pat yourself on the back," he says. "I don't disagree, though."

"Well, you have to admit, a day at the zoo is more or less the opposite of spending the day mediating an argument between two clients who can't decide whether to redo their rumpus room in giraffe print or zebra," I point out as I reach across the table to steal one of Dax's fries.

He pushes the whole basket toward me. "What the hell is a rumpus room, anyway?"

"It's what pretentious snobs call a game room." I refrain from admitting I'm one of those pretentious snobs, or at least I used to be. Now, I'm not so sure.

"I'm proud of you, Lisa."

The comment startles me, and I study my corndog as though the explanation might be skewered on a stick and wrapped in deep fried cornmeal. "How do you mean?"

"For coming up with this idea."

"The zoo or The Test?"

"Both. I meant The Test, but I've gotta admit I haven't visited the zoo for years. Not since I was six and I came here for some special freebie day for underprivileged kids."

His face darkens just a little, and I'm not sure whether to ask about it or change the subject. The old Lisa would gloss things over to keep the conversation bright and easy.

That's not what I do. "Was it not a good experience?"

He shrugs and glances out over the aviary beside us. We've chosen a table where we can watch birds flitting from branch to branch, and his gaze follows a golden-breasted starling being pestered by a cluster of speckled mousebirds.

"Part of the deal was that poor kids got a free backpack," he says. "It was supposed to be a back-to-school thing, I guess. I was so proud of that damn backpack, and I wore it around the zoo all day like a fucking superman cape."

I smile at the mental picture, though there's a twinge of uneasiness in my gut. I remember my own mom lecturing us—Cassie, Missy, me—about setting aside part of our allowance to donate to poor kids who needed school supplies. It seemed like a charitable idea at the time, but now I bristle at the memory of her words. At the self-serving place they may have come from.

"Did something bad happen with the backpack?" I ask softly.

He turns away from the birds and looks at me. "I was standing there licking my free orange popsicle and watching the polar bears when this group of boys comes walking up beside me." His voice sounds distant and a little hollow, but his eyes hold mine. "I heard one of them snickering and then he said, 'Look, there's one of those welfare kids with the ghetto backpack.'"

"God." I wince. "Kids are so horrible."

He clears his throat. "I didn't realize he was talking about me at first. I had no idea—" His voice dries up there, and he shakes his head for a second before glancing back at the birds. "Anyway, it felt pretty shitty."

"Did you throw the backpack away?"

There's a flicker of irritation in his expression. "Hell no. I couldn't afford to be prideful. Not then, anyway."

I nod and start to reach across the table for his hand. At the last second, I realize that might feel like pity, and I know it's the last thing he wants right now. Instead, I grab another french fry. "That's really lousy. I'm sorry that happened to you."

The words sound cliché and hollow, but I hope he knows how much I mean them. That I really do care, and that I hate more than anything that at some point in my life, I've probably been one of those elitist kids. Not a bully, mind you, but certainly a self-congratulatory princess doling out hand-me-downs with little thought about how it felt to be one of the recipients.

Dax reaches across the table and gives me a small smile. "Hey. Thank you."

"For what?"

"For listening. For bringing me here today and making it a great experience." The smile gets bigger. "And for fucking me senseless last night."

I smile back and curl my fingers into his. "You do that a lot, you know."

"Fuck you senseless?"

"That, too. But I meant changing an uncomfortable subject by saying something crass."

He studies me a moment, then nods. "Good point. You're probably right."

"I'm not complaining. Just an observation."

He gives my hand a squeeze then lets go and picks up his second corndog. "Come on. Let's finish eating so we can get to the Warty Pig demo."

I laugh and pick up my phone, which just buzzed with an incoming text message. "That's Sarah," I report. "She says thanks again for helping with yesterday's field trip to Helping

Paws."

"It was fun." He grins. "Junie and all her friends seemed to love it."

"She had a total blast."

He laughs and swipes his corndog through the ketchup again. "I loved how she taught that big Rottie mix to roll over. Duke's been skittish around everyone else, but Junie just walked right up and melted his heart."

"She has that effect on everyone." I take a bite of my corndog and suddenly remember something I've been meaning to ask him. I chew quickly and dab my mouth with a napkin. "Speaking of Junie, are you familiar with the Diamonds and Opals Charity Ball?"

Dax gives me a guarded look and grabs a fry. "That fancy black tie gala they have in the Pearl District every year? What does that have to do with Junie?"

"The proceeds this year are going to the Association for Down Syndrome Research," I explain. "Simon's on the board of directors, and he bought tickets for the whole family, but it turns out Missy and her husband can't make it."

I let the words hang there for a second.

"Are you wanting to go?" he asks.

I nod and take a sip of my iced tea. "I was already planning on it, but now there are a couple of extra tickets. I was wondering if you might like to join me."

There, I said it. Well, I didn't say it quite right.

"Actually, no," I say. "Let me rephrase that. I know you probably wouldn't like to go, since you told me before you hate dressy events."

That gets a smile from him. "You have a good memory."

"Right. And I guess what I was trying to say is that I would love it if you'd accompany me to the ball. I'd really like to have you with me."

Dax takes a bite of his corndog and chews thoughtfully.

"It's the last Saturday of the month, right?"

I don't ask how he knows, though I'm curious. I also wonder if he realizes that's the final day of The Test. If I say nothing, maybe he'll forget.

"It's at the Markham Center this year," I say. "Black tie only, of course."

"Of course." He nods and sets down his corndog before taking a slow sip of soda. "I accept."

"You do?"

I probably sound like a kid on Easter morning, but I don't care. I'm giddy that Dax is going with me. "I promise I'll make it painless. We can hang out with Simon and Cassie and mock snobby rich people all night if you want."

That gets a smile out of him. "You know how to push my buttons," he said. "The good ones, I mean."

"I'm a big fan of your buttons."

He laughs and picks up his corndog again. "Okay, then. Want me to pick you up in a limo at six?"

"You don't have to do that—"

"Nah, it'll be fun. I rarely take the opportunity to be a wealthy jackass. Might as well give it a shot."

"Thank you, Dax." I reach across the table and squeeze his hand. "Really. This means a lot to me."

"I know it does," he says. "That's why I said yes. Also, why I'd say yes to just about anything you asked me, especially when you do it with your shirt unbuttoned and that pleading look in your eyes."

I glance down to see all my buttons are, in fact, fastened. I meet his eyes again to find him grinning. "Okay. Maybe it's just you."

Something flutters in my belly, and I do my best not to break into a little happy dance at the table. "Maybe so," I say as I reach to steal the last french fry.

...

We walk into the ballroom of the Markham Center to a symphony of sounds. Literally, a symphony. There's an eight-piece orchestra playing in the corner, while tuxedoed waiters float around the room like they're doing the waltz with their platters of artfully arrayed shrimp puffs.

I smooth my hands down the skirt of my black silk chiffon gown, a four-thousand-dollar dress I scored for mere pennies from Rent the Runway.

Not that anyone here needs to know that.

Judging by the number of designer labels I spot in this crowd, there's more money in this room than in Bill Gates's checking account. Ladies in beaded evening gowns laugh a little too loudly, everyone jockeying for attention. It's the place to be seen for wealthy Portlanders, and I have to admit, it's a scene I know well. I spot a former client across the room and give a friendly wave before looping my arm through Dax's.

"You doing okay?" I ask.

"Yeah, fine, why?" He glances at me and offers a smile made stiffer by the way he's clenching his jaw.

"Because you keep yanking at your tie like it's strangling you."

"It *is* strangling me."

I reach up and adjust it for him, then stand on tiptoe to kiss the corner of his mouth. He gives a sexy little growl and pulls me against him, going in for a deeper kiss.

I'm breathless by the time I pull back. "Better now?"

"Much." He grins, a real one this time.

"Come on," I say. "Let's grab a glass of wine. Maybe that'll help."

"I don't know if I can swallow with my neck in a noose."

"I'm sure you'll give it your best shot."

I slip my hand into the crook of his elbow again as we head toward the bar on the south end of the ballroom. I survey the crowd, keeping an eye out for familiar faces.

"Your sister's here, right?" Dax asks.

"Cassie texted to say they're running late," I tell him. "The board roped Simon into giving a last-minute speech, so they're hiding out in the car scribbling notes or something."

"Or something." He grins and glances down at me. "Is that code for making out in the back seat?"

I laugh and clutch his arm tighter. "I see you've caught on quickly."

"I think it's cool," he says. "How they're so into each other."

"I agree." I step around a tuxedoed waiter and wonder which part of their couplehood Dax admires. The crazy-hot chemistry? The easy conversation? The fact that it's so clear that Simon has Cassie's back, and vice versa?

Or maybe it's the whole package. I can't help wondering if Dax wants that for himself someday, the way I want it for me.

I hold back on saying any of that, since a charity ball swarming with well-heeled masses is hardly the place for that sort of conversation. "They're a great couple," I agree benignly.

We step around a massive ice sculpture that's an architectural model of the new community center they're hoping to build with funds from this event.

"Pardon me," I murmur to two ladies dripping with diamonds and swirling in a cloud of Hermes Perfume 24 Faubourg. The stuff sells for $1500 an ounce, so I can't say I'm disappointed when one of them grabs my arm.

"Oh my goodness, Lisa Michaels," the redhead gushes. "I was just telling Ashley here what a fabulous job you did redesigning Peter and Bridget's penthouse over in the West

Hills."

"Yes, of course," I say, delighted to be recognized for a job I'm pretty darn proud of. "How *are* Peter and Bridget?"

"Fabulous," the blonde says again, and I wonder if it's the only adjective in her vocabulary "They're at their place on St. Kitts right now, having a little escape."

"Well deserved," I chirp, though I have no idea what two trust-fund billionaires without jobs would need to escape from. I smile anyway and gesture to the redhead's diamond choker. "What a gorgeous piece."

"Thanks." She strokes her fingers over the fat rock at the center and leans in conspiratorially. "Max bought it for me to make up for the fact that he spent fifty-grand without telling me on his last boys' getaway. You know how it is."

"Of course," I say, though I have no earthly idea how it is. Not from personal experience, anyway.

The brunette extends a well-manicured hand. "I'm Tiffany," she says. "I love the work you did for Peter and Bridget's place. The color choices in the formal dining room were exquisite."

"Thank you so much," I say. "Aubergine and coral really pop in the right setting."

"I don't suppose you have a card?" Tiffany asks. "I'm looking to redo my place in Lake Oswego."

"Absolutely." I fish into my beaded handbag and extract a business card from my monogrammed silver holder. "My sister and brother-in-law live right there on the lake, so I'm over there quite a bit. I'd love to swing by sometime and take a look at the space."

"Wonderful," she says with a little finger flutter that's equal parts friendly and dismissive. "I'll be in touch. Ciao."

"Ciao," I echo, thanking my lucky stars she didn't do that stupid trendy air kiss that got so popular with Portland socialites a couple of years back.

As the ladies wander off, I feel Dax watching me. "What?" I ask, not sure how to read his expression.

"You." He gives a small smile, but I can't tell how to read it. "You really know how to work a crowd like this."

"Thanks." I'm not entirely sure that was a compliment, but I'm choosing to take it as one. "Schmoozing at events like this can be important for my business."

"I can see that." He smiles and leans down to plant a kiss at the edge of my ear, and I shiver with pleasure. "And I can see right down to your belly button in that dress. Have I mentioned it's fucking fantastic?"

I grin and reach up to finger one of the beaded straps. "What, this old thing?"

He laughs and grabs my hand again. "Come on. Let's go get that wine."

We've almost reached the bar when an elegant blonde steps in front of us. She wears a glittering red Versace gown and a smile so big I could count her teeth.

She reaches out to touch Dax's arm, and I have to fight the urge to bite her hand.

"Dax, honey." She smiles wider, and I think maybe I can see her kidneys. "It's so good to see you again."

Judging his tense expression, the feeling is not mutual. His arm stiffens in my grip, and I glance up to see he's clenching his jaw again.

He turns and looks at me with a stony expression, and I know.

It's *her.*

"Lisa Michaels," he says slowly. "I'd like you to meet Kaitlyn Whitaker."

# Chapter Eighteen

## Dax

The shock in Lisa's eyes would be completely undetectable to anyone who hadn't spent the last month watching for clues to her state of mind.

"It's lovely to meet you, Kaitlyn," Lisa says with so much poise and charm she's practically oozing it.

My ex-girlfriend extends her own manicured hand, and the two ladies exchange the most civilized, frosty handshake in the history of female handshakes. "Likewise," Kaitlyn says, eyeing Lisa up and down. "Lovely dress. Naeem Khan, right?"

Lisa nods and tosses her hair, cool as can be. "That's right. Yours is beautiful, too."

"Mmm, thank you. It's Versace."

"Yes, I recognize it. From their fall collection, yes?"

I grit my teeth, understanding this as part of the mating dance that's done between the social elite at events like this where everyone's trying to figure out how some new introduction might benefit their career or social status. Three years with Kaitlyn made me familiar with it, but that doesn't mean I enjoy it. The women chatter on about their shoes and handbags and I start to tune out until I hear my own name.

"Dax, sweetie." Kaitlyn rests a hand on my arm, and I wonder if Lisa recognizes it's a power play. Probably not, since she has no way of knowing my ex was never an arm toucher or a pet name user during our time together. Kaitlyn's shark smile is another indicator, and she flashes it at me before continuing. "How do you and Lisa know each other?"

I glance at Lisa, waiting to see what she'd like to volunteer. How she'd like to frame our relationship. "We met at the Driftwood Room," Lisa says, taking charge of the conversation and steering it back to safer turf. "Have you been there?" Lisa asks. "Their Sazerac is to die for."

"I haven't yet, no." Kaitlyn's guarded expression says she's weighing how crucial this might be to her social standing. "How does it compare to the Sazerac at Pepe Le Moko?"

"Mmm, they use George Dickel rye and a splash of hibiscus tea simple syrup, for starters. Very fresh and unique."

I start to tune out again, wishing like hell we'd made it to the bar. I could go for two fingers of Jack Daniels neat right about now. I consider slipping away, or maybe signaling Lisa that I need some air. Then again, maybe a connection with Kaitlyn could benefit her business somehow. Far be it from me to fuck that up for her.

I've lost track of the conversation again when I hear Kaitlyn's voice addressing me.

"So, Dax," she says. "I hear you're kind of a bigshot now."

The words are barbed hooks, but the bait is tough to resist. This is what I've wanted, right? A chance to rub my ex's face in the fact that I've moved on to better things?

One of those better things saves me by resting her hand on my arm and giving a reassuring smile. "Dax's company was just mentioned in *Oregon Business* magazine," Lisa says, giving my arm an almost imperceptible squeeze. "Maybe you saw the article?"

"Maybe." Kaitlyn glances at me, calculating. She picks up the event program off the bar table next to us and flips it open. "Well, then. Maybe you'd like to bid on one of the silent auction items? On behalf of the company, of course."

She holds the program open in front of me, and I glance down at the sea of words. Letters swirl in a chaotic alphabet hurricane that makes no sense at all. Words, so many goddamn words. A cold sweat prickles my forehead, and my pulse starts to hammer in my ears.

I know this feeling. I know it so fucking well and I hate it.

"Uh—" I jab a finger at one collection of indecipherable letters and shrug. "Sure. I think I'll bid on that."

Lisa glances down at the page, and the two women titter with laughter. Kaitlyn covers her mouth in feigned politeness, but not before I see traces of a smirk. "Oh, Dax," Kaitlyn says. "You're useless."

Still giggling, Lisa gives a little head shake. "Come on, now. Men are always a little hopeless when it comes to that sort of buying decision."

Kaitlyn takes the program back and shakes her head at whatever the hell I've pointed at. "Yeah, but it would be just your dumb luck he'd end up winning it. Then you'd be stuck."

Rage is bubbling hot and sour in my chest. I'm not sure where it's coming from, but their words bounce off my eardrums like stones thrown at a brick wall.

*Useless.*

*Hopeless.*

*Dumb.*

There's not enough air in the room. I yank at my tie, desperate to get out of here. Desperate to escape the money and the condescension and the fake laughter and clinking glasses.

I mumble something about needing air as I turn and stalk out of the room. Laughter echoes behind me, and my mouth fills with the sour taste of orange popsicle and shame.

I don't stop walking until I find myself out in the parking lot. Standing there with my back against the building, I gulp huge lungs full of air until my breathing begins to slow.

"Dax?"

I turn to see Lisa approaching, her expression pinched with worry. "Are you okay?"

She totters a little on too-high heels, and I hate myself for feeling judgmental instead of protective. But goddammit, who the hell chooses footwear that practically begs for a broken ankle? People who give a shit about appearances, that's who.

"Go back inside," I say. "I need a minute."

Twin creases appear between her brows, and she glances uncertainly back over her shoulder. "Is this about the cufflinks?"

"Cufflinks?"

"The ones you pointed at in the catalog. The four-thousand-dollar solid gold Star Wars cufflinks. I'm sorry, I thought they seemed a little ridiculous, but I guess—"

"Ridiculous." The word is bitter and sharp on my tongue, and I spit it onto the pile of judgements that have been hurled at me throughout my life.

"Dax?"

I turn to see her brow furrowed in confusion. "Why are you here, Lisa?"

She looks at me uncertainly. "I just wanted to be sure you're okay," she says. "Everyone around us got kind of worried when you went shoving through the crowd like a Walmart customer on Black Friday."

I know she's trying to lighten the mood, but something about the joke makes me angrier. She's standing here in her gazillion-dollar dress and gazillion-dollar shoes like someone who's never set foot in a discount store. Never had to shop the sales or scramble for every goddamn penny.

*You don't have to, either, dumbass. Not anymore.*

I might have money now, but that doesn't mean I don't remember what it feels like to go to bed hungry. To feel the scornful eyes of people like Kaitlyn and Lisa and all the rest of them.

I clear my throat, recognizing that I need to be very, very careful right now.

"You'd better go back inside, then." There's a dark note in my voice that I wish wasn't there, and I scrub my hands down my face in hopes of resetting my attitude. "If you care so damn much what everyone thinks of you, you'd better not leave the gossip squad alone for too long."

Her expression shifts from concern to irritation. She folds her arms over her chest and stares me down. "What is that supposed to mean?"

I should just apologize for being an asshole, put my arm around her, and take her back inside to grab that glass of wine.

But a lifetime of shame and anger and judgment are bubbling in my gut, and I can't seem to stop them from frothing up through my stupid mouth. "It means I don't belong here, Lisa. And clearly, you do."

She stares at me. "You say that like it's a bad thing."

"Maybe it is."

Her eyes narrow. "What are you driving at?"

I could stop this now. Just shut the fuck up and quit talking.

But I don't. I pivot to face her, angrier than I have any right to be. "Look, you're the one who decided to change your life," I growl. "To let go of the trappings of your pampered, elitist world and become a better person."

She reacts like I've just slapped her, and maybe I have.

Never in the weeks we've known each other have I been so blunt in my judgment. I open my mouth to apologize, but she's already shaking her head.

"The Test was an experiment," she says. "A temporary way for me to try new things and learn about myself. I never planned to become my own polar opposite for all of eternity."

The word *temporary* rings in my head, bouncing off my brain's soundwaves with *useless* and *hopeless* and *dumb* until all of them blend into a shrill scream that makes my hands ball into fists.

"Congratulations, then," I tell her. "You've spent your thirty days slumming it in the ghetto. Done your charity work, rubbed shoulders with the unclean, gotten fucked in an alley, all that good stuff."

She flinches at that last part. I should stop, but I can't. "You're officially done with The Test," I say. "There's nothing keeping you here."

"Clearly," she mutters, then winces. "I didn't mean—"

"No, I know what you meant." I shake my head, knowing damn well I have no reason to respond in anger, when I'm the one who started this. But I can't seem to stop.

"Go on, Lisa. Go back to your perfect, polished little life."

"What?"

"We're done now, right? Thirty days. That was the agreement."

Tears fill her eyes. That's the worst part. I wish she'd yell or scream or kick me. Tell me I'm being a selfish asshole. All of that would be true.

But instead, a single tear spills down her cheek. "Why are you doing this?" she whispers. "I don't understand where this is coming from."

I don't understand, either. Or maybe I do. It's about where *I* come from, which is vastly different from Lisa's world. How did I not realize that before? What kind of idiot entertains the idea that an uneducated dumbshit from the wrong side of the tracks could ever have any place in a world like Lisa's?

*You. You're the dumbshit.*

"It was fun while it lasted, but I think we're done now," I say slowly. "Don't you?"

"Done," she repeats as she stares at me. "With us, you mean."

I nod once, not able to say the words. It takes me a full ten seconds to force them up past the knot in my throat. "This was temporary, anyway. You said so yourself."

"In the beginning it was," she says slowly, eyes still glittering with tears. "But I thought we were both starting to feel something else. Something different."

I shake my head and glance away, knowing I can't say what I need to with those green eyes boring into my soul. "You thought wrong."

I can't look at her. I need to end this now. This conversation, this charade, this stupid hope that I could ever have something long-term with someone as smart, beautiful, and sophisticated as Lisa.

*You'd only fuck it up anyway.*

My chest aches like someone's standing on it, and I can only imagine how much worse it would be if we let things go longer. If I got attached, if I fell in love—

*You're already in love.*

"No!"

I turn to see her blinking at me like I've just cursed in church, which is the least of my offenses. I take a step back, needing to put more distance between us. Needing to commit fully to what is hands-down my dumbest act of self-preservation in my whole history of misguided decisions. I yank at the goddamn tie, ready to rip the fucking thing off my throat.

"We're too different," I growl. "Isn't that clear by now?

Hasn't it been the whole time we've been doing The Test? It was the whole point, wasn't it?"

She shakes her head slowly as another tear slips down her cheek. "We're more alike than you think." She reaches up and dashes the tear away, and I want to pull her against my chest. To fix what I've just smashed to pieces.

A door slams nearby, and she whirls around to see who's it is. It's just a waiter coming out for a smoke break, and her face is washed with relief as she turns back to face me.

"Thank God it's not my sister," she says. "Or Kaitlyn or—"

"Go back inside," I say again. "The last thing you want is for people to see you out here with me."

She stares at me for a moment then shakes her head. "Dax."

I don't know what else she planned to say. She presses her lips together, tears still glittering in her eyes, but they aren't falling anymore. I fold my arms so I don't reach for her. So I don't make this harder on us both.

She nods once. "Fine. If that's what you want."

It's not what I want. Not at all. But I can't make myself say those words out loud.

Or any words at all as she turns and walks away, her expensive heels clicking on wet pavement.

Shame and anger and self-pity foam up in my chest like a toxic volcano.

*Of all the stupid things you've done—*

Stupid. That's exactly what I am. It's all I'll ever be. Surely Lisa knows that? It's better this way, it has to be.

She disappears into the building, and the door slams shut behind her, a hard, metal clang that echoes off the bricks behind me.

I close my eyes and lean back against the cold, damp wall, hating myself more than I have in my entire life.

# Chapter Nineteen

## Lisa

It's Sarah who finds me in the bathroom crying.

I love my sisters more than anything, but for some reason I'm relieved it's her instead of them.

She sits down beside me on the red plush chaise that looks both luxurious and absurd in a room where women go to pee.

"What happened?" she asks.

Without waiting for an answer, Sarah slides a hand into her little black handbag and pulls out a small silver flask. She offers it to me without comment, and I give a choked little laugh-sob.

"That's why," I say out loud as I screw off the top and knock back a mouthful of gin so strong it may as well be turpentine. I wipe my hand over the back of my mouth and hand the flask back.

"Why what?" she asks.

"Why I'm glad it's you," I say. "Missy would have handed me a cross-stitched lace hankie and a Belvedere martini, and

Cassie would have tried to make me laugh with dirt jokes. Not that I wouldn't appreciate it, but sometimes a girl just needs to drink straight gin in a bathroom while wearing a four-thousand-dollar rented dress."

Sarah laughs and takes her own small sip from the flask before tucking it back in her purse. "I wasn't sure they'd have anything at the bar that costs less than my monthly car payment."

"Good guess. A woman who plans ahead." I shake my head, chastising myself for not doing exactly that. Not with gin, but with Dax. How the hell did I think this was going to end?

"For the record, I'm not working tonight," Sarah says. "In case you're worried about me drinking and looking after Junie."

I glance at her, startled. "Is that what everyone thinks of me? That I'm such a judgmental bitch?"

It's Sarah's turn to look startled. "What? No! That's not what I meant at all. I was just—"

"Sorry. I was just venting."

I take a deep breath and scrub a tissue across my cheeks, leaving dark smears of mascara on it. I can only imagine what I look like.

*You care so damn much what everyone thinks of you…*

I wince at the memory of his words, and Sarah gives me a sympathetic smile. "I take it you and Dax had a fight?"

I nod, wishing for another nip from the flask. "Yeah. He said we're too different. That we come from different walks of life."

"That's true enough," she says. "But don't they always say opposites attract?"

"Attract trouble, maybe," I mutter. "That's about it."

She studies me for a moment, then shakes her head. "Nah, there's more than that between you. I saw it the other day on the field trip. The way he looked at you like you invented pepperoni pizza and ESPN. The way he hung on every word you said. That's more than sex, my friend."

I sigh and shake my head. "I don't understand why he blew up like he did. One minute we were joking around with his ex-girlfriend about some stupid thing he pointed to in the program, and the next minute he's stalking out of the room like I kicked his dog."

The reminder of Dax's dog story sends a flash flood of guilt coursing through me.

So does Sarah's creased brow. "Did you use that word, by any chance?" she asks. "Stupid?"

I stare at her. "I have no idea. Why?"

"Well," she says slowly, choosing her words with care. "It's just that adults with disabilities can be really sensitive about that. About judgement words or phrases that make them feel dumb."

My brain starts to spin, and I'm pretty certain it has nothing to do with the gin. "Disabilities? What are you talking about?"

Sarah frowns. "I'm sorry, I just assumed—I thought you knew?"

"Sarah, what on earth are you talking about?"

She bites her lip, hesitating. "The paperwork I gave you guys before the field trip," she says. "The way Dax asked you to fill his out for him."

"Right, he said he had to take an important call…"

"Sure, maybe. But later when you left the room, I asked him to read the waiver form out loud for some of the other volunteers. It was clear right away he was dyslexic, so I stopped and moved on to something else."

"Dax is dyslexic?"

How on earth did I not know?

Sarah's studying me like she's wondering the same thing,

but she's too polite to say it. "I'm pretty sure, yes," she says. "I assumed it was something you'd talked about."

I shake my head, dumbfounded. "I had no idea."

"I guess that doesn't surprise me, now that I think about it."

"What do you mean?"

Sara shrugs and fiddles with the zipper on her purse. "I did a lot of coursework on adult dyslexia when I was working on my special ed degree. Unfamiliar fonts—like the ones on those forms for the field trip—those can be especially challenging for adults who have a tough time with reading."

*Or the fonts in the program.*

I clear my throat. "Apparently, he didn't want me to know."

My head is reeling, and I can't wrap my brain around this. We were as intimate as two people can be. He told me about his childhood dog and the story about the laughing boys at the zoo, but he didn't see fit to share something this important?

"Don't feel bad," Sarah says, resting a hand on my arm. "It's really common for adults with learning disabilities to keep it to themselves. They don't want to look stupid."

Stupid.

*You're so fucking smart. Why is that such a turn-on?*

Dax's words from our time in the Oregon Adventure exhibit rearrange themselves in my memory, like puzzle pieces clicking together. Did I make him feel dumb? Like he couldn't be himself with me?

"Don't blame yourself," Sarah says, reading my mind. "With dyslexic men in particular, there's a lot of shame involved. With someone they care about, they're afraid of looking weak or unworthy in a new relationship."

I shake my head, stung by the words almost as much as the fact that I didn't know. "We're not in a relationship," I murmur. "Not anymore. He made that pretty damn clear."

Sympathy clouds her eyes, and she slips an arm around me. "You're sure?"

I nod. "He said we're both ready to be done with this." I swallow hard, hating the tightness in my throat. "And I said okay."

Sarah gives me a squeeze. With the other hand, she reaches into her bag and pulls out the flask. "Here. Keep it. You need it more than I do."

"Thanks." I take a hearty swallow, feeling sadness and shame burn down my throat with the gin. I wonder if I should find Dax and apologize.

*No. He chose not to let you in. He made it clear he's done.*

"It was only meant to be temporary anyway," I murmur, lifting the flask to my lips again. "Maybe it's best just to let things go."

Sarah says nothing at first, but there's pity in her eyes as she nods. "Sometimes it's fine to be single while you figure out who you are and what you want."

"Cheers to that," I say with no cheer at all. I pass the flask back, knowing how badly we both want to believe that.

Wishing like hell I did.

Wishing, more than anything, that I hadn't fallen hard for Dax.

# Chapter Twenty

## DAX

I move through the pat-down like a zombie, holding up my arms so the guard can frisk me before I shuffle through the metal detector in a daze.

I've visited my brother in prison a million times before, but it feels different this time.

"You look like shit," Paul says the instant he sits down across from me at the battered metal table.

"Thanks," I mutter. "You're fucking ugly, too."

Brotherly affection at its finest.

Paul laughs and leans back in his chair, arms folded behind his head. "Love you, too, baby brother. So, who pissed in your cornflakes?"

I can't believe this is the conversation we're having less than five seconds after I arrive for my weekly visit. Then again, it's all I've thought about for the last twenty-four hours. I take a deep breath, considering whether to confide in him.

*Keeping secrets is part of what fucked you over with Lisa.*

"It's no big deal," I mutter at last. "Broke up with some chick I've been seeing."

"Some chick." My brother snorts like that's the funniest thing he's ever heard. I have to admit, the words sounded dumb coming out of my mouth. "Man, you're the worst liar ever. You wouldn't be sitting here acting this fucking miserable over 'some chick'"—he lifts his hands in dramatic air quotes—"who didn't mean shit to you."

I sigh, not wanting to get into this, but not sure I have any choice. "Look, it's no big deal. We were seeing each other for a while, but now we're not. End of story."

That's such a blatant lie I can't even look at him when I say it. From the disgusted snort across the table, I can tell he's not buying it. "Whatever, dude. What was her name?"

"Lisa." My chest tightens as I say it, and I hate myself even more. "Lisa Michaels."

"Lisa Michaels," he repeats. "What did you do, fuck her sister or something?"

"What? No! Are you crazy?"

Paul barks out a laugh. "Maybe. I'm in prison, aren't I? Think it's too late to do an insanity plea?"

The fact that my brother is being so jovial about this makes me feel shittier. Like it's possible to feel worse. What kind of asshole shows up and dumps his relationship woes on a guy who's been stuck behind bars for the last three years?

"I didn't fuck her sister," I say. "Can we please talk about something else?"

Paul shrugs and drops his hands to the table, spreading them wide on the chipped black metal. "Sure thing, man. What do you want to talk about?"

"I don't know. Read any good books lately?"

That gets a good laugh out of him, and I find myself smiling a little, too. It's been our inside joke for years. One nobody but a couple of dyslexic degenerates would find funny.

"Hey, you remember that time the principal sent notes home with us about how we were a couple dumbshits who couldn't read and needed to be in special classes," Paul says. "But we couldn't read the goddamn forms and neither could dad, so we ended up shoving them in the burn pile?"

"Yeah," I mutter, darkening again. "Great childhood memories. Almost as good as that time dad shot our dog."

My brother stops laughing and frowns at me. "What the fuck are you talking about?"

I roll my eyes and rub my palms across the table. "Killer. You remember Killer, right?"

"Of course, but Dad didn't shoot him."

"The hell he didn't," I growl. "He loaded him up in the truck and drove away with his gun. When he came back, no dog."

Paul looks at me, then shakes his head. "Man, that's really what you thought all these years?" The pity in his eyes makes me feel worse, which is saying something, since I already feel like shit. "Dad always had his gun, idiot. That doesn't mean anything."

I roll my eyes, not willing to let my brother sugarcoat things. "So what do *you* think happened?"

"I don't *think*," he says. "I *know*. I was there. I was hanging out at the bar with a fake ID when the old man showed up asking if anyone wanted to buy a wolf dog."

I stare at him, not sure whether to believe the story. Part of me wants to. Wants it desperately, more than anything. "What happened?"

Paul shrugs. "Bartender said sure, his kid had been bugging him for a dog. Traded fair and square for a fifth of Jack."

I stare at him while my brain spins with this new version of history. I want to believe him. I do believe him. Why would he make this up?

"Why didn't you say anything? To me or to dad or—"

"What, and risk getting my ass whooped for hanging out at a fucking dive bar at sixteen?" He shakes his head. "Besides, how the hell was I supposed to know that's what you thought? You never said a damn thing."

He's right. My habit of hiding shit that makes me feel bad isn't my most admirable trait, but I'm still processing the dog thing, so I don't have time to think about it.

"Killer didn't die?"

"Well, probably at some point," Paul says. "It was more than twenty years ago. Dogs don't live forever."

I grunt and scrape my hand over my chin. "Hell, he probably ended up in a dog fighting ring or something."

"Jesus, man." Paul reaches across the table and whacks me on the side of the head. That gets the attention of a guard, who starts toward us with a frown. I wave him off.

"It's cool," I assure him. "Brotherly love, not assault."

The guard shakes his head. "Watch it."

"Roger that." I salute him, then turn back to Paul. "What is your problem?"

"You, dumbshit."

He's the only person who can call me that and not have me take it personally. Am I an asshole for being so touchy about that? It's just a word, after all. Words aren't exactly my strong suit.

Paul is still talking, so I order myself to pay attention. "What is it with you, anyway?"

"What do you mean?"

"You always have to come up with the worst-case scenario. You know what your problem is?"

I sigh. "No, but I figure I'm about to learn from a guy doing six years hard time for robbery."

"Yeah, well sometimes the people who've screwed up the most have the best lessons to offer."

Okay, he has a point.

"Can't argue with that," I mutter, rubbing a hand over the spot where my chest has started to ache. Has been aching for the last twenty-four hours. "Fine. What is my problem?"

"You can only see the worst-case scenario. There's no happily-ever-after as far as you're concerned."

"So?" Not a very mature response, but it's all I've got.

"Why'd you and your chick split up?"

"Because she's a high-society snob who thinks I'm worthless and stupid."

Paul rolls his eyes. "Did she actually say that? Did she tell you, 'Dax, I'm a snooty socialite who's too good for you, and oh, by the way, you're too dumb to pour piss out of your own boot?'"

I fold my arms and try to stare him down. "Not in so many words, no."

Paul shakes his head again, but he's starting to look mad. "You jackass. You've got every chance in the world right now to have everything—the cool job, the money, the smart, hot girl."

"I never said she was hot or smart."

"Please," Paul mutters, studying my face so intently that I want to glance away. "You wouldn't be this broken up about her if she were a dog-faced idiot."

I grunt again to concede the point, so Paul keeps talking. "You've got everything going for you, and you're going to piss it all away because you're too fucking chicken to believe you could have any of that. To believe you deserve it."

I open my mouth to argue, then close it again. Is there any chance he's right? That my jailbird thief of a brother has a point?

I swallow hard, not liking that direction of thought. Not wanting to admit I might be wrong.

I also don't like the words on the tip of my tongue, but I

say them anyway. "I'm scared," I whisper. "So fucking scared, man."

It's the first time I've said those words out loud to my brother. Maybe to anyone, ever. I expect him to laugh out loud, but instead he reaches across the table for an awkward sort of fist-bump.

"I know," he says. "Believe me, I know. We lost Mom, then Pop, then Dana. You think I don't know how much it sucks to make up your mind that you're gonna care enough about someone that it'll rip out your fucking guts to lose them?"

I nod, swallowing back the tightness in my throat. He knows. My brother might be a criminal, but he's pretty damn wise. "I guess."

Paul sighs and leans back in his chair. "Look, man. You've got to at least try. Maybe you can't have it all, but maybe you can. You sure as fuck have opportunities I'll never get. You've gotta make something of that shit."

As pep talks go, it's not the most eloquent. It's nothing you'll hear in a self-help seminar, but those words resonate with me. Or maybe it's Paul's encouraging expression.

"You think I could fix things?" I ask. "Maybe have another shot with Lisa?"

This time, he does laugh. "You're asking for love advice from guy who's been showering with a bunch of other dudes for the last three years?" He shakes his head and cracks up at his own joke, but then his expression softens. "Yeah, man. I do. I really do."

It's enough for me. That hope, that stupid nugget of hope. Seeing it laid out before me on this battered table is like the best gift I've ever been given.

"Thanks, man," I tell him. "I really hope you get out on appeal soon."

"Why, so you can hit me up for love life advice all the

time?"

"Yeah," I say. "We'll sit around drinking coffee and talking about our feelings."

"Maybe form a book club," he adds, and we both bust out laughing again.

As the guard signals us to wrap things up, I stand. So does Paul, and we embrace each other in one of those awkward bro hugs that's only permitted at the end of a visit.

"Now go on," he mutters, slapping me hard on the back. "Go out and get your girl back."

I nod and look him in the eye, determined to do whatever the hell I can to follow his advice. "I'll give it my best shot."

# Chapter Twenty-One

## LISA

"Is that a hickey on your neck?"

Missy sits down beside Cassie in the steam room and gives our baby sister her most judgmental, older sister stare.

Cassie blushes and touches a hand to her neck. "Maybe? It was our nineteen-month dating anniversary last night."

I fight back a twinge of unwelcome envy as Cassie looks between us with a love-dazed puppy dog expression.

Missy rolls her eyes. "What are you, sixteen?"

"Hey, don't judge a girl for getting laid." Sarah adjusts herself on the bench across from them, tucking the corner of a fluffy white towel so it's wedged between her boobs. "I think it's great she's marrying a guy who makes her look all googly-eyed and satisfied."

"Or a guy who springs for a girls' getaway like this." I squeeze Cassie's hand. "Seriously, this is the sweetest birthday gift I've ever gotten from someone who wasn't even my official brother-in-law yet."

"You're welcome." Cassie's smile falters just a little. "Sorry your birthday month has been a little rough."

I shrug like it doesn't matter, even though my heart squinches up like a raisin in my chest. "It's for the best. Besides, I wouldn't have gotten to do this if I were still doing The Test."

"Really?" Missy frowns. "Was Dax such a hard-ass about not letting you do stuff like this?"

"No, that's not it at all." I stretch out my bare legs to admire my new pedicure, my heart twinging again when I remember the time Dax nibbled my toes in bed, making me giggle so hard I almost passed out. "He was never a jerk about things. He didn't make rules about what I could and couldn't do. Just steered me in a different direction sometimes, that's all."

"Well, I'm glad it's over," Missy says. "Back to the old Lisa again."

Cassie looks thoughtful for a moment. "I don't think so." She studies me for a long time, those green eyes so intense I feel like a soil sample under one of her high-powered microscopes. "You're different now. More centered."

"I agree," Sarah says. "More balanced. Regardless of what a jerk Dax turned out to be, I think we can thank him for that."

"He's not a jerk." My reply sounds weak, and hearing his name makes my throat hurt. I ignore it and focus on adding a few drops of lavender essential oil to the contraption next to the steam vents. "It's fine, really. I'm doing okay."

"Of course, you are." Cassie pats my hand, and I know what she's thinking. She and Simon went through a rough patch like this before they got together for good.

But it's different for Dax and me. There won't be a happily-ever-after for us. If he hadn't made that clear in the alley during the Diamonds and Opals event, he's sure as hell made it clear with his silence in the week since then.

I wish that didn't sting so much.

"Well, anyway," Cassie says. "I love that you're volunteering at the dog place now."

"And that you did karaoke with us the other night," Sarah adds.

"And your recipe for homemade marshmallows is out of this world," Missy adds with a little less enthusiasm. "Even if you did make us assemble that filthy fire pit instead of roasting them indoors like civilized people."

I smile at the compliments, proud of how far I've come. They're right, of course. I have changed, at least a little. I'm still me, obviously. Still fussy and pretentious and way too focused on appearances.

But appearances are my business, so I won't apologize for that.

I will, however, embrace some of the things Dax introduced to my life. Laughter and bravery and the ability to take myself less seriously. I owe him a debt of gratitude for that.

Thinking about him again has my throat pinching painfully, so I change the subject. "Isn't it just about time for our massages?" I glance at my watch before remembering I left it in the pocket of my robe outside the steam room.

"Yeah, we should probably get out," Cassie says. "Our appointments are in a couple minutes."

"I do hope they can do a good Shiatsu massage," Missy says.

"I suppose this isn't the sort of place that does a happy ending massage?" Sarah jokes. "I'm having a dry spell right now."

We all stand up and file out of the steam room to fold ourselves into the big, plush robes provided by the resort. I adjust the chignon at the back of my head, eager for an hour of feeling good.

*You know who else made you feel good?*

"Shut up," I mutter to my subconscious as four attendants walk in wearing crisp white polo shirts bearing the resort's logo. A pretty brunette consults her clipboard and steps toward me. "Are you Lisa?"

"That's right," I say. "You're Annabelle?"

"Yes, I'm your massage therapist today. If you'll follow me this way."

I cinch my robe a little tighter and move behind her down the plush-carpeted hallway filled with soothing Enya music. At the end of the hall, Annabelle turns and points me through a small door. Her expression is a little odd, but I don't think much of it as I step into the waiting area that separates the couples' massage suite from the treatment room for hot stone massage.

"Right in here," Annabelle chirps as I walk through the door.

I take two steps and freeze. There, on the bench between the rooms, is a familiar figure. A *huge* familiar figure with tattooed arms jutting out of the sleeves of his too-short robe. He wears a shaky smile and socks that clash horribly with the plush robe, and he's the best damn thing I've ever seen.

"Dax," I choke out when I finally get air in my lungs.

He stands up, looking big and uncomfortable, but determined. He glances at me, then at Annabelle, who hovers nervously by my shoulder.

"I hope this is okay," she whispers. "Your sister told me—"

"It's fine," I tell her. "Thank you."

"Oh, good," she breathes. "I—um, I'll be right outside if you need anything."

And with that, she pivots and hustles through a door. As soon as it closes behind her, I turn back to Dax. We're alone in a waiting area filled with flickering candles and ferns. A small fountain bubbles in the corner, and he takes a step forward.

"Lisa." His voice is husky, and he's staring at me like he's never seen me before.

Maybe he hasn't. Not without makeup. "Hello."

"Lisa. God, you're beautiful." He takes a shaky breath. "Wait, let me start over. This isn't about what you look like."

He steps closer, almost close enough now to touch me. But he doesn't, and I'm glad. Not that my whole body isn't screaming for it, but it's his words I want most right now. Why is he here?

"Look, I fucked up." He clears his throat. "As apologies go, I know that's pretty piss-poor."

I smile a little at that. "It's okay."

"No, it's not okay." He rakes his hands through his hair and shakes his head. "I got so hung up on bringing you into my world that I didn't stop and think about how selfish that was. That I owed you the same damn courtesy."

His words touch me, but I keep my shoulders squared. I don't want him to see how hurt I still am. "You don't owe me anything, Dax," I say softly. "We were clear from the beginning how things would be."

"That's just it." He shakes his head again and reaches out to touch my hand. "Things changed. For me, anyway. I don't know when I realized I was falling in love with you, but it scared the holy living shit out of me and I panicked. I panicked and said stupid things, and I'm sorry."

"Wait, what?"

I replay his words in my head, trying to figure out how we got from *I fucked up* to *I love you*. Is that what he just said? Or was it *loved*, past tense, as in he doesn't anymore—

"I can see the wheels turning in your brain, and it's one of the sexiest things about you. Your brain, I mean." He smiles and squeezes my fingers. "Don't look so shocked," he adds. "Yeah, I love you. I fucking said it."

There's a defiant expression on his face, but something vulnerable, too. Like he's daring me to argue, to laugh at him, to walk away.

I do none of those things. I twine my fingers through his and squeeze hard enough to keep the tears at bay. "Dax—"

"I love you," he says again, and I realize I could never tire of hearing those words. Not from him, anyway. "I love the Lisa Michaels who goes camping and sings karaoke, but I also love the Lisa Michaels who hoards handbags and knows the difference between a crudité and charcuterie."

"The veggies and meats and cheeses play off each other nicely, so it's best to have both."

*Shut up, Lisa.*

Dax just laughs. "And that's the other thing. I love that you're smart. Though the fact that you spent a month sleeping with a dumbshit like me calls that into question."

"You're not dumb, Dax." The passion in my voice is so fierce, even he looks surprised. "Anyone who can start his own company from scratch—who can overcome barriers like poverty and loss and dyslexia and—"

"You know?" His eyes widen, and it's the first time I've seen him look totally unsure in this conversation.

"About the dyslexia?" I nod and tighten my grip on his fingers. "Yes. Sarah figured it out," I say slowly. "And it doesn't make me think less of you. In fact, it makes me love you more."

It takes him a second to register what I just said. When he does, his whole face breaks into a grin. He pulls me close, his chest warm and solid through the terrycloth of our robes.

"Yeah, I fuckin' said it," I murmur, doing my best to imitate his earlier line as his lips find mine. "I love you, too."

His kiss is deep and dizzying and leaves me tingling all

the way to my toes. When he draws back, we're both a little breathless.

"I'm so sorry," he says. "I got scared and ran. But if you give me another chance, I promise my days of being a chickenshit are over. I'm in this for the long-haul."

"Me, too." I clasp his hands tighter, breathing in his familiar smell. "And I'm sorry, too."

"What the hell for?"

"For treating you like a tour guide to the seedier side of life," I say. "For making you feel devalued."

"You didn't." He shakes his head, his expression adamant. "You never did. I'm the one who let myself get caught up in that bullshit story."

I tip my head back to study him, in awe of this man standing in front of me. He's the same Dax I fell in love with, but there's a rawness there I never saw before. A bravery and openness that steals my breath away.

"What do you say?" he asks. "Want to give this a shot?"

"You and me, you mean?" I grin and nod. "Definitely."

"Then let's get Annabelle back in here."

I raise an eyebrow, not sure if he's suggesting some crazy threesome thing to cap off The Test.

But as soon as he opens the hall door, Annabelle bounds in and smiles at us. "I take it you decided to do the couples' massage class?"

I look at Dax. "Couples' massage class?"

"Yep," he says. "I want us to learn something new together. Something that'll make us both feel good for a long time to come."

I smile and stroke a finger over his palm. "One of many things," I murmur as we turn and follow Annabelle into the couples' suite.

# Epilogue

## DAX

"Would you like a gourmet s'more, sir?"

The tray appears with a flourish in front of me, but I'm more interested in the woman holding it.

Catching Lisa by the waist, I pull the s'mores tray from her hand and set it on the workbench behind me. The scarred wood surface is covered with a linen tablecloth and a vase of lilies, but it's a workbench all the same.

Three well-dressed art enthusiasts skirt around us, helping themselves to a s'more en route to the next cluster of sculptures on display.

Lisa giggles as I press her against the wall for a kiss. "Did I ever tell you that you look fucking sexy in an apron?"

"Sir!" She pretends to be appalled, but the flush in her cheeks tells me she loves it. "We're at a gallery opening!" she scolds with mock indignation. "What sort of savages would engage in carnal relations at a sophisticated event celebrating arts and culture?"

"The kind of savage who holds his own art gallery opening in a steel fabrication warehouse," I growl, kissing her again before I let her go. "And the sexy woman who came up with the idea in the first place." I give her butt a fond squeeze. "Thanks again."

She beams and glances around at the crowd. "I'm really impressed by the turnout."

"Me, too." I survey the room, a little dumbfounded by the number of people who showed up to gawk at steel art constructed by some no-name welder who just happened to make a wolf sculpture. And a tiger. And then a dancer and enough other random objects that Lisa finally said it was a shame to keep them cooped up in a warehouse where no one else could see them.

I've gotta admit, it's been cool to have other people checking out my work.

A wet nose jabs into the back of my hand, and I look down at the baleful eyes of my dog. Well, *our* dog—mine and Lisa's. Part bloodhound, part great-Dane, she looks like a steer with a thyroid condition. One of her long ears has gotten stuck under her lacy pink collar, and I untuck it as gently as possible.

"Hello, Miss Kitty," I say. "How's the party treating you?"

"She's been a little naughty," Lisa says. "I caught her begging Cassie for canapes."

"The smoked salmon or the ones with the butternut squash and goat cheese?"

"The salmon, of course," she says. "But Cassie gave her one of each to see which one she liked best."

I pat the dog on the head. "Atta girl. A lady with a refined palate."

Lisa laughs and picks up the tray of s'mores. "I should finish handing these out to guests," she says. "Then I have a surprise to show you."

I perk up at that, wondering if she bought another sexy lingerie set. I've become a big fan of La Perla over the last year. "Does the surprise involve you taking off your clothes?"

Lisa laughs and gives me a haughty expression. "As a matter of fact, it does."

"That's my favorite kind of surprise."

She twirls away, and I watch her circulate around the warehouse handing out mini s'mores and compliments and smiles for everyone. People in her path light up as she passes, and my chest swells with pride that this amazing woman has agreed to spend the rest of her life with me.

That's right. I proposed last month over a big dinner party at our place. Her whole family was there, and I popped the question between the amuse-bouche and the hors d'oeuvre courses. I got down on one knee like a damn gentleman and asked her to fuck me senseless for the rest of our natural lives.

All right, I was more eloquent than that. And she said yes, which made me the happiest son of a bitch to ever walk the earth.

"Hey, Dax." Junie sidles up with a smile on her face and a mini s'more in one hand. "I really like your art."

"Thank you," I say. "And thanks for coming tonight, too."

Junie grins wider. "Did you hear I've been driving a car?"

"I did. Simon said you were doing drivers ed classes. How's that going?"

"Great." She beams. "And maybe after I get my license, I can get a motorcycle license, too."

"That would be awesome," I tell her, meaning it. "Let me know if you need a lesson or two."

"Deal." She looks down at the dog, who is eyeing her s'more with lust-filled eyes. "Can I take Miss Kitty for a walk?"

"Sure thing. Her leashes are on that hook by the door.

Pick whichever one you want. I think the orange one you like is on the end."

"Nah, she's wearing the pink lace collar, so she needs the pink lace leash to match. Everyone knows that."

I laugh as my dog trots off with Junie, all loyalties forgotten as she fixes her eyes on the s'more.

I turn my attention to a pair of guests who step up to ask me about my inspiration for one of the pieces. After that, the editor from some art magazine—the same guy we met at the show with the wolf photos—stops by to talk about connection between CoolTanks manufacturing and my artwork. I'm so focused on doing the artist thing that I lose track of Lisa for a moment.

The second she steps up behind me, I know she's close. I sense her somehow, and I turn to see her beaming up at me with a mischievous glint in her eye. "Hey, sexy. Got a sec?"

"I've got all the sex you want."

She giggles and grabs my hand. "Come on. There's something I want to show you."

She tows me toward my private office, weaving through scattered pockets of people staring at the sculptures. When we get to the room, she shuts the door behind us and leans against the edge of my desk with a grin.

"You know how I said I had a spa appointment this morning?"

I nod and tuck a strand of hair behind her ear, mostly an excuse to touch her. "Right, at that place downtown?"

"Yes, but I might have fibbed a little." She smiles. "Not about the appointment, but what it was for."

"What do you mean?"

She grins and slides her apron off over her head, then sets it aside on the desk. "Well, I went to get this."

Before I can say anything, she turns around with her hands braced on the desk. My dick surges as she hikes up her skirt, and it takes me a second to realize it's not an invitation.

"Oh my God," I breathe, mesmerized by her left butt cheek. More mesmerized than normal, that is. "You got a tattoo?"

"Uh-huh." She looks over her shoulder and gives me a smile that's almost shy. "Do you like it?"

"I love it." I reach out to touch it, but remember at the last second to keep my hands off fresh ink that's still healing. "It's a wolf," I say rather unnecessarily.

"It is," she says. "I took the artist a picture of your sculpture and asked him to draw something inspired by that." She slides her skirt back down and turns to face me. "I wanted it to be a surprise."

"I can't believe you did that," I breathe. "It's amazing."

"I always used to say tattoos were tacky," she admits. "Then I met you."

I cross my arms, making sure to flash my own palette of ink. "Aren't you the same woman who said you wanted to lick each of my tattoos, one by one?"

She grins and nods. "Exactly. I wanted my own to remind me that the things you can't imagine yourself doing—the things that make you scared or scornful or judgey—those can end up being what you love most of all."

"Your tattoo is great," I say, eager for another glimpse of that delectable backside. "Let's see it again."

She turns and lifts her skirt once more, and I admire the ink up close. It's small and tasteful, but exquisitely done. The perfect combination of artsy and edgy, beautiful and raw.

In other words, everything I love about my bride to be.

She drops her skirt again and turns back around. I pull her into my arms and slide my hands into her hair, marveling that she's mine. That we get to go home together tonight. And the night after that, and the one after that.

I kiss her hard and deep and so fiercely that we're both

breathing hard by the time we come up for air.

"So, you like it, huh?" she says. "The tattoo?"

"Love it," I murmur. "It's bootylicious."

She dissolves into giggles again, and I smooth my hands down her sides, so damn happy I could explode. "I love you, Lisa Michaels."

"I love you, too, Dax Kensington. And I can't wait until we're alone together. I want to do bad things to you."

Her words send a jolt straight to my cock, and I grip her hips a little tighter. "Well," I say softly. "Did I ever show you the shower in this place?"

She smiles and cocks her head to one side. "I may have seen it a time or two."

"Hmm," I say. "Maybe you need a refresher course. A fresh introduction to the seedier side of life."

She giggles again and nods. "Show me the way."

"My pleasure."

We turn and walk from the room side by side, fingers laced together in a perfect fit.

It's exactly how we'll be for the rest of our lives.

# Acknowledgments

Huge thanks to readers who loved *The List* and who wrote to me in droves wanting to know if Lisa's story would be next. I'm grateful to you for buying my books and making it possible for me to forge a career out of playing with imaginary friends.

So much love to my critique partners and beta readers, including Linda Grimes and Kait Nolan. You make me a better writer and a better human.

A zillion hugs and kisses to Meah Meow for kicking ass as both a pet sitter and an author assistant. Thank you for improving my life dramatically over the last year.

Thank you to Karen Fernandez Vickers for naming Miss Kitty the dog, and to all the street teamers in Fenske's Frisky Posse for being the best support team and sounding board an author could ask for.

Big bunches of gratitude to Michelle Wolfson of Wolfson Literary Agency for being my advocate, business partner, and friend these last ten years (which is crazy, since obviously, we're both still in our mid-twenties. Did I start publishing books at fifteen?).

Thanks bunches to Liz Pelletier of Entangled Publishing, and to the entire Entangled team for all your hard work making my books the best they can be and getting them out to the masses. I'm grateful to Jessica Turner, Melanie Smith, Heather Riccio, Christine Chhun, Debbie Suzuki, Curtis Svehlak, Riki Cleveland, Shayla Fereshetian, and anyone else on the Entangled team who I might have inadvertently forgotten here. Love you guys!

Endless thanks to my family for all the love, support, and laughter over the years. Dixie and David; Russ and Carlie; Cedar and Violet—I couldn't do this without you.

And thank you to Craig Zagurski for being my hero and partner in all the best ways. Love you, hot stuff.

# About the Author

When Tawna Fenske finished her English lit degree at 22, she celebrated by filling a giant trash bag full of romance novels and dragging it everywhere until she'd read them all. Now she's a RITA-nominated, *USA Today* bestselling author who writes humorous fiction, risqué romance, and heartwarming love stories with a quirky twist. *Publishers Weekly* has praised Tawna's offbeat romances with multiple starred reviews and noted, "There's something wonderfully relaxing about being immersed in a story filled with over-the-top characters in undeniably relatable situations. Heartache and humor go hand in hand."

Tawna lives in Bend, Oregon, with her husband, stepkids, and a menagerie of ill-behaved pets. She loves hiking, snowshoeing, standup paddleboarding, and inventing excuses to sip wine on her back porch. She can peel a banana with her toes and loses an average of twenty pairs of eyeglasses per year. To find out more about Tawna and her books, visit www.tawnafenske.com.

*If you love erotica, one-click these hot Scorched releases...*

## HIS FOR THE WEEK
### a novel by Alice Gaines

Sex columnist Désirée "Rae" Knight is in a bind—and not the kind she usually likes. Her newest assignment, and possible big break, is an article for her magazine on the sex resort that just opened. The only problem is it's couples only. Although she writes about having red-hot sex, she's been single longer than she'd like to admit. Enter her coffee shop crush, who she's been secretly ogling every morning. Trouble is, he doesn't know she exists.

## BIG CATCH
### a *Dossier* novella by Cathryn Fox

Former New York stockbroker, Brayden Adams takes one look at Alyssa and knows she needs to relax. He'd known the feeling himself, until he and his best friend, Tyler, left the fast life behind when they inherited a hotel and fishing business in Antiqua. Now they live a relaxed island life and share everything. But Alyssa makes him question everything he knows.

## HOLD ME HARDER
### a *to Have and to Hold* novel by Renee Dominick

PR exec Natalie Lindgren thought she was past her days as a submissive. But that was before she ended up at one former Dom's ranch for her sister's pre-wedding getaway—and discovered the best man was a former Dom, too. How was she going to get through the weekend? Especially when it seemed unlikely that she'd end up on top...

Made in the USA
Columbia, SC
05 January 2021